Julian Sturgis

Comedy of a Country House

Vol. I

Julian Sturgis

Comedy of a Country House
Vol. I

ISBN/EAN: 9783744786423

Printed in Europe, USA, Canada, Australia, Japan

Cover: Foto ©Andreas Hilbeck / pixelio.de

More available books at **www.hansebooks.com**

COMEDY

OF

A COUNTRY HOUSE.

BY

JULIAN STURGIS,

AUTHOR OF

"THRALDOM," "JOHN MAIDMENT," ETC.

IN TWO VOLUMES.

VOL. I.

LONDON:

JOHN MURRAY, ALBEMARLE STREET.

1889.

COMEDY OF A COUNTRY HOUSE.

CHAPTER I.

A YOUNG man came over the hill. He was walking on one of those public field-paths which lead the landless wayfarer through the homely beauties of England, and make him too for his little hour a lord of the happy land. He went with long strides and with the vigour of youth, but without the elasticity of the first morning hours. One would have known from his gait that he had been walking all day. His strong, hob-nailed boots went steadily forward; his stick was no longer swung in careless fashion; his slouched hat was pushed a little back from his forehead. He tramped along in business-like way, like

a vagabond to the manner born. Over his
left shoulder and under his right arm a thick
red blanket was rolled and fastened. Invisible
in the inner pocket of his old shooting-coat
were lighter luxuries—a comb, a clasp-knife,
and finally that tried companion of the
English gentleman in every climate and all
circumstances of life, his for richer for poorer,
the last thing from which he parts except his
life—the tooth-brush.

The young man came over the hill, and
followed his little path across the wide,
shallow valley; but where the path began to
rise again he left it, and climbing more
quickly through a little hanging wood, came
out above the trees on to a bare grassy knoll,
which gave a wide view of all the country
round. There he sat down with an inarticu-
late murmur of satisfaction, stretched his tired
legs before him, and raised his eyebrows at
the view. It was a brown landscape, for
the month was brown November; but no
monotony of colour could hide the beauty of

the land. A wide plain lay open at his feet, a plain to him who sat so high above it, but really a wide stretch of gently swelling land, of fertile but not heavy soil, of curves and lines delightful to the eye; an open country, but with copses and coverts not a few, with grass and ploughed fields in fair proportion. The ploughed fields were of a warm, reddish brown; the bare hedges of a colder, darker hue; and the brightest specks were seen where the yellow-brown leaves of the young oaks still clung to the boughs. The pomp of summer had gone, with its dark deep leaves and yellow corn; but if the scene of its splendour was now bare and brown, the brown was varied enough, and there was no look of bareness in the woods, which seemed to clothe the gentle slopes like the fur of some soft brown beast.

The traveller was fond of the face of nature and of the face of England. He looked with much contentment across the wide expanse. His eyes wandered with enjoyment, but they came back again and again to one place, where, miles away, the tower of an unseen castle rose above its more majestic trees. He regarded this tower with a whimsical air, half annoyed and half amused. He had walked all day for a sight of it, and, when he saw it, he burst out laughing. It was his. His was that castle, which seemed to raise its head that it might announce its presence and its importance to the world. His were all these well-tilled fields and pleasant woods, as far as and farther than his eye could see. And much of the land through which he had tramped since dawn was his too. He looked at the good country dirt upon his boots and laughed again, thinking that even that was his, and again that the solid earth on which he sat was his to its very centre. He was young and fanciful, and he liked to amuse himself with such fancies. And then he remembered another large estate in another county, with its appropriate residence, and reports of landed properties

comparatively unimportant, and a yacht
which was lying somewhere. And then too
in London there was the family mansion,
majestic in a majestic square; and somewhere
in less lordly districts a lot of land, on which
houses were thickly built, and which, as he
had heard, would enable him to smile at the
lowest possible prices of agricultural produce.
But it was not at low prices that he smiled
like a Cheshire cat or a member of the
Cobden Club. He smiled at himself and at
the strange part which he was called upon to
play. He was young and fanciful, and easily
moved to laughter; and he could not but be
interested and amused by the new, and in
its way brilliant, part which he was expected
to play. But here lay the element of
boredom. He was expected to play the part,
and to play it according to the well-known
traditions. Nothing was more firmly fixed
than the proper rules of conduct for the young
heir; and, as he looked at the tower, which
seemed to be peering over the trees and on

its side solemnly looking for him, he felt an
unmistakable repulsion and an unseemly
levity arising within him. Were the days of
his freedom over and the boyhood to which
he clung for its simplicity and joy? It
amused him to think of himself competing
with that castle in dignity; it amused him, but
it vexed him too; and, even while he laughed,
there was vexation in the sound of his
laughter. He knew that in that stately
abode was a country-house party gathered in
his honour; he knew that he ought to have
been at home to receive them twenty-four
hours before; he knew that his uncle was
there prepared to point out certain duties for
his doing, and that his aunt was there to urge
him perhaps to duties even more important.
He was by no means sure that he objected to
these duties, and yet—and yet—— Over
the wide landscape the tender light of evening was diffused. It was time to go down
and encounter that country-house party, and
to surrender himself to the appointed duties

of his position. There were people there whom he would like to see, but the people were a country-house party. "A country-house. party," he said to himself; "it is terrific."

All the vagabond in the boy rose against the momentous words. He would have another night of freedom, come what would. He kissed his hand to the expectant tower, and went down the further slope of the knoll. He whistled as he walked back to the village, where he had dined at midday. Nobody in the village knew him, though, for aught he knew to the contrary, he might be owner of it all. He supped well as he had dined well; and he amused himself by trying to excite the curiosity of the landlady, who was evidently surprised at seeing neither a bicycle nor a tricycle, neither a photographic camera nor a closely-strapped bundle of samples. He encouraged in her a dawning belief that he was something "in the detective line,"—a belief which was due to a happy notion that

detectives went about in disguise, and that to
attract universal attention by a slouched hat
and a Rocky-mountain blanket was but the
natural conduct of a member of the secret
police, a tribute to the dramatic necessity of
disguise. A brother of an Anglican Order,
who had recently visited the village, clad in
a brown robe and with a rope round his
waist, had excited in the good lady a like
lively suspicion.

After supper the vagabond took to the
road again. If the end of his liberty were
near at hand, he would have a deep draught
for the last. The night was fair, the wind
was light and westerly, and for a November
night there was but little cold. He turned
away into the fields, trespassing boldly on
his own tenant's land, skirted a little wood,
lest some officious keeper of his own might
seize him as a poacher, and soon found the
suitable hay-stack which he sought. He got
over the hurdles which surrounded it, rolled
himself close in his thick red blanket, and lay

down to leeward of the stack. There he would sleep, as he had slept before, close to the kindly earth, beneath whose bare surface the life of the next year was stirring now. He liked to be so close to his mother earth. He pulled some handfuls of hay and rolled them in his cashmere scarf for a pillow; and so he lay and watched the watching stars. And then he fell asleep, and slept soundly till the first chill of dawn.

CHAPTER II.

One of the dreaded country-house party, and perhaps the most terrible of all, was Lady Jane Lock. On the morning after that night, which her disappointing host had spent beside the haystack, Lady Jane was in a pleasant room on the first floor of the Castle, but not in a pleasant humour. She was cross; and, when she was cross, few things annoyed her more than her dear friend Susan Dormer's habit of smiling. Mrs. Dormer now lay on the sofa with her most provoking air of placidity. The sofa suited her; the room suited her. Indeed, she had chosen the room for her boudoir on account of its double doors and its southern aspect; and, since she was the aunt of this absurdly rich young man, and had determined to keep

house for him until he married, these seemed
good reasons for choosing the best room in
the house as her own. Southern aspects and
double doors were recommended by her
doctor; and to see her friend Jane "a little
put out" did her good too, though this was
no part of the doctor's prescription.

Lady Jane stood exceedingly erect and
stared out of the window without any
apparent pleasure in the south; and indeed
the pleasant light, which came in, was not
becoming to her, for her high colour, tempered
by a liberal supply of violet powder, would
have produced a better effect had she turned
her back to the window. This great truth
was very clear to Susan Dormer, whose own
skin retained to a remarkable degree the
clearness and softness of girlhood. But Lady
Jane was not thinking of her own looks, but
rather of the broad acres which stretched
away before her eyes. She was a judge of
parks; she had married two daughters to
them; but there was no park so much to her

taste as this of Langleydale. What timber and what a ring-fence! She knew the length of that fence.

"I'd better have gone to Bolitho," she said, still staring out of window. "The Duke was most pressing," she added after a minute, since Mrs. Dormer kept silence.

"Dukes are never pressing," murmured Mrs. Dormer from the sofa.

"It is no good at all," said Lady Jane.

"What is no good, dear?" asked Susan innocently.

"No one has been in more country-houses than I have," said Lady Jane, as if she challenged contradiction.

But her friend only sighed. "How bored you must have been, poor dear!" she said with a soothing tone.

"But never, never before has such a thing happened to me. My host never appearing at all, and not a word of explanation, let alone apology!"

"I know it is very disappointing, dear,"

said her friend, as if she sought to comfort her, " when all your plans were so nicely laid too."

" My plans !" cried Lady Jane, starting as if at the flick of a whip. " I have told you before, Susan, that I will allow nobody to speak to me as if I were a worldly match-making mother. There is no character of which I have such a horror."

" Did I say anything, dear, about match-making ?" asked her friend. " We all know you are not worldly, I am sure. Your poor dear Delia's marriage showed that."

It was evident that this instance of her unworldliness failed to comfort Lady Jane Lock. She turned and looked straight at her friend, who met her with a candid smile. " No one could say that it was worldly of you, Jane," said Susan Dormer, " to marry your poor dear Delia to a scrub of a curate."

" You know as well as I do, Susan, that Delia's husband is a Vicar. It is exceedingly likely that he will be made a rural dean."

"How charming!" murmured Susan; "a rural dean! It's quite Arcadian. But it was nice of you, dear," she continued with gentle emphasis, "to marry her to somebody who was—who was nobody."

"Adolphus's family is one of the oldest in England."

"Really? How very nice! And is it really true that they only have mutton twice a week?"

"Certainly not," said Lady Jane Lock; "it is a detail, a ridiculous detail, but the vicarage, a most lovely vicarage embowered in roses, is in the heart of a famous sheep country. I see nothing to laugh at."

"Nor I, dear."

"Delia does not require much butcher's meat."

"She is so right," said Mrs. Dormer, with a marked access of seriousness; "my doctor says so. Twice a week is quite enough."

"My daughter can have mutton every day, if she wish."

"Yes, dear Jane; but who would wish to have mutton every day? You know, dear, I was only saying how nice and unworldly it was of you to marry poor dear Delia to a penniless nobody!"

"I have told you again and again, Susan, that, if Adolphus's mother had been a man, she would have been fifteenth baronet."

"Yes, dear; but if she had been a man, she wouldn't have been his mother."

Lady Jane Lock was taken aback. Her friend's remark appeared to her equally indelicate and unanswerable. She sat down abruptly with a movement of disapproval and took up the *Morning Post*.

"Any way, Jane," said Susan Dormer presently, "I think we can do better for Elizabeth."

Lady Jane Lock perceptibly concentrated her attention on her paper.

"Of course things suit me very well as they are," continued Susan, looking comfortably around her, "but I know very well that they can't stay like this. The poor dear boy is so absurdly rich, and he is not at all clever, except at books and that sort of thing —he can't escape long."

The *Morning Post* rustled in Lady Jane's hands, and a sound came from behind the paper, which was suspiciously like the word " coarse."

"Of course, dear, as you say," continued Mrs. Dormer placidly, " of course the poor dear boy is sure to be married by somebody. So why not Elizabeth ? I am all for Elizabeth. I do like her so much ; she is so like her dear father."

"Not in the least," said Lady Jane, who had intended, like Iago, to speak no more. Mrs. Dormer ignored the contradiction. She smiled and said, " Elizabeth has real beauty ; she is not like poor Delia."

"Many people," said Lady Jane. emphatically, "admired Delia more than any of her sisters."

" Did they, dear ? "

"I cannot help it," continued the other loftily, "if the general taste of the day is inexpressibly vulgar."

"Oh, poor dear Elizabeth!" murmured Susan Dormer; "that is too bad, Jane. I should never think of saying that Elizabeth looked vulgar. Perhaps she is not in the *most* refined style; I go with you as far as that; but not vulgar—oh no, I really think not."

Lady Jane Lock laid down the paper and looked at the friend. She opened her mouth, but shut it again with determination. After a time she asked this question : "Susan, do you think that Lord Lorrilaire is coming here at all ?"

"Yes," said Mrs. Dormer, "I am sure that the poor boy will come. He is odd, but he really would have let me know if he was not coming at all; he knows that I asked people."

"Does he know that I am here ?"

Mrs. Dormer smiled. "I think that he

suspects, poor dear," she said; "he is not suspicious, but really after London—well, I for one hope that we shall make the match."

She reposed, smiling. On her large fair face there was no sign that she was aware that she was not making the most agreeable speeches to her friend. And yet she knew Jane so well that she knew exactly where to touch her with effect; and, when she was administering a little wholesome dig, then she smiled. Her smile was peculiar, for her mouth was so small in comparison with her smooth calm countenance, that a smile produced hardly any effect on her expression. A little extra amiability was suggested, as she smiled and said that she hoped that they would make the match.

"I cannot tell you," said Lady Jane, stiffening herself like a grenadier, "how much I detest this talk of making matches. I regard it as little better than impiety."

"Oh!" said Mrs. Dormer, faintly.

"Some marriages are made in heaven," said Lady Jane Lock, with due solemnity.

"And others in country-houses," said her friend. She was rather shocked when she had said it, and added promptly—"that is what Clara Chauncey says."

"It is worthy of her," said Lady Jane, sharply.

"Yes, dear," said Mrs. Dormer; "she is so clever."

"Clever, yes! You know my opinion of Mrs. Chauncey."

"Oh yes, dear."

"A most dangerous woman!"

"Oh yes, dear," said Mrs. Dormer, smiling; "but not dangerous to us. Poor dear Clara cannot interfere with our little plan."

Lady Jane made no comment but an impatient snort.

It was really an unlucky morning for Lady Jane Lock. There were many questions which she was eager to ask; but on the other hand she felt that she could not open her mouth without a fresh sacrifice of dignity. Here was such a good opportunity of a really useful talk with her friend; but it seemed to her, as it often seemed to her, that her friend was either so stupid or so perverse that she could get nothing from her but annoyance. She was not even sure that Susan really believed that young Lord Lorrilaire would really come; and if he were not coming, she knew that she ought to be angling for a renewed invitation to Bolitho; she wondered if the duke would ask her again. She was just making up her mind to start afresh with Susan, and to try to lead up by a new path to those questions which she longed to ask, mere careless questions about the disposition of the property and such matters, when she heard the outer of the two doors opened, and the voice of Sir Villiers Hickory asking if he might come in.

"Oh yes, do come in and amuse us," said Mrs. Dormer; "we are so dull. I am told to be amused after breakfast." The voice of

Susan Dormer had no other tone so solemn as that in which she always referred to the advice of her doctor.

Sir Villiers came in, looking brisk and business-like. He was a very good-looking man of his years. He had preserved his light figure and his clear eyes, which were almost colourless. For the rest, he was fresh-coloured, with that rather mottled look which ruddy men acquire with time, thin-lipped and firm of jaw and chin. He was a slender, erect and alert elderly gentleman, and he was admirably dressed. He gave thought to his dress, determined that as an old man he would be neither fop nor sloven, and determined too that his clothes should not look as if he thought about them. He was now dressed, as he held that a man ten years younger than himself should be dressed in a country house on a week day; he had allowed himself the benefit of those ten years after due deliberation, having decided, and quite rightly, that he looked at least ten years younger than his contemporaries at the Club.

If Mrs. Dormer received Sir Villiers graciously, Lady Jane made no great effort to hide her annoyance.

"I never expect to see men in the morning," she said; "why ain't you killing something?"

"We can't always be killing," replied the gentleman sharply; "we leave that to the ladies." It was a pretty speech, but not without a slight tartness, a mere suspicion of irony. Lady Jane only acknowledged it by a sniff; but Mrs. Dormer was charmed.

"You are a dear man!" she said.

"Never mind that," said he. "I have come to ask if you haven't heard anything of the boy."

"Not a word," said Susan, smiling.

"It'll be awkward if he don't turn up," he said.

"He always turns up," said she placidly.

"It is settled," said Sir Villiers, "that Palfrey is to make a big speech at Langstone.

and I have asked him in Archie's name to
stay here for the affair."

"But, my dear Villiers, I thought that the
poor dear boy was a Radical or a Republican,
or something."

"It doesn't matter a fig what he *was*. He
was nobody, and might have been a Shaker
or a Peculiar Person for what anybody cared.
But now he is somebody, and now it does
matter. Langley Castle has always been the
centre of the Tory party in the county, and
Archie must give his money and entertain
the spouters and stumpers like other people.
Palfrey will certainly come, and Archie must
not only entertain him here, but must preside
at his meeting." He went to the fireplace
and put his hand on the bell. "May I
ring?" he asked.

"Of course, Villiers; and we will see if
anybody comes."

"They come when I ring," he said.

The bell was pulled with decision, and
answered with promptitude.

"Has Hawkins heard from Lord Lorri-laire?" asked Sir Villiers.

"No, Sir Villiers," said the footman, "but his Lordship have arrived."

"What?" cried Sir Villiers.

Lady Jane leapt in her seat, and even Mrs. Dormer turned her head.

"Yes, Sir Villiers, he came in this morning through the window of the long drawing-room, when the housemaids were doing it. His Lordship went straight to the bath-room."

"Well? Where is he now?"

"His Lordship is asleep."

"In his room?"

"Yes, Sir Villiers."

"Did he bring his luggage?"

"His Lordship's luggage is at Langstone, at the Blue Boar."

"The wrong house!" said Sir Villiers sharply; "a Radical pot-house! Tell Blake to send a cart for the luggage at once—at once!"

" Yes, Sir Villiers ; " and the man departed.

When the two doors had been closed, Sir Villiers looked sharply from one lady to the other.

" We've got him," he said.

" Yes," said Mrs. Dormer softly, smiling on Lady Jane Lock, " *we* have got him."

Lady Jane wished not to understand, wished to be indignant, but, before she could decide what it were best to express, she, much to her own surprise, gave vent to an abrupt crude laugh.

CHAPTER III.

PRESENTLY young Lord Lorrilaire would wake from his dream of the sheep-fold and of the patient stars to find himself stretched on his patent bedstead, and under his own majestic roof. It seemed almost as likely that he would wake a little later from his dreams of freedom and of happy friendship to find himself an engaged man and a patent Conversative politician. His uncle, Sir Villiers Hickory, if his view was somewhat narrow, saw all which it included, with a remarkable keenness. He was not embarrassed by doubts; he was a man of decision; he had established the useful habit of having his own way. His aunt, Mrs. Dormer, had a large store of that immovable obstinacy, which is only found in women, and in women

of a lethargic and most amiable temperament.
And, finally, Lady Jane Lock, though she
disliked the reputation of a successful match-
maker, was at least a most fortunate mother-
in-law.

Nevertheless, it was not the wishes of these
relations and friends which were the chief
danger of the young man, but rather the
mood which now possessed him—a mood
dangerously acquiescent. He was not de-
ficient in character, as the popular phrase is.
On the contrary, he had more character than
could be set forth in pieces by a few sentences
of even the most cunning analyst. He had
always been a clever boy, clever and kind-
hearted. His mother, who had lost her
husband soon after the birth of this their only
child, had retired to a small place in the
country. There she had become by degrees,
and in spite of her gentle methods, the lead-
ing philanthropist of the neighbourhood; and
thence she had sent to London at long
intervals certain works of fiction, which

betrayed on every page her tenderness of
heart, her timid love of religion, her delicate
literary taste, and her sublime ignorance of
the world.   By the side of this gentle mother
her little boy had trotted into cottages,
and ceased his cheerful babble for a moment,
wondering that there was sorrow in the world.
His mother had loved to soften the little heart,
which did not need it.   The first money
which the little hand had held was put into
it that it might be given to the poor.   So
Archie Rayner had learned, before he was
breeched, that he must look about for those
who needed help, and help them as well as he
could.   This seemed an uncommonly simple
affair to the little boy, and, so long as it went
no further than carrying half his pudding to
the little lame boy at the lodge, it was
simple enough.

Archie went straight from home to a public
school, and after the first night, when he cried
himself to sleep, he found a pleasure quickly
growing in the companionship of other little

boys. Playing with zeal, working without lassitude, and idling less than most of his fellows, he had not much time to remember that there were any less fortunate lads in the world; and, as his intelligence grew rapidly and he began to question this and that, the village and its wants, of which he read in his mother's letters, seemed so small in the distance that he could scarcely help laughing at his mother's seriousness. It was like the little scraps of good advice which she put in her postscripts, and for which he loved her, though he laughed. Indeed, he laughed a great deal, being given to laughter, and a popular and pleasant person. And then, when he was sixteen years old, his tutor, who was what was called in those days a Philosophical Radical, was struck by one of his questions, which sounded intelligent, invited him to join his Debating Society, lent him some books, and administered to him an occasional sententious maxim as a stimulant to youthful thought. Thereupon a new world

seemed to open before the boy, who had not
caught the true scholar's interest in the
structure of the Greek and Latin languages.
He read eagerly, and, as he read and thought,
his childhood's philanthropy rose strong
again within him ; and the questions. religious
and political, which he asked himself and his
tutor, tended more and more to take the
practical shape—how to help the poor. It
became apparent at once that this was no such
simple affair as it had seemed in the far-off
days of pennies and pudding. Presently he
wrote home a boyish pompous letter to his
mother, questioning her methods, and more
than hinting that his researches were likely
to lead to the conclusion that she was pauper-
izing the parish. His mother was immensely
proud of his letter, and not at all disturbed by
the criticism, having that power, so common
in mothers, of combining an excessive admiration of the cleverness of her child with
complete indifference to his opinions.

But the Debating Society and the stimu-

lating tutor soon showed this young scholar
that there were other interesting political questions besides that of helping the poor.   What
was the object of politics ?   He asked his tutor
this question ; and his tutor put into his hands
for answer Mill's "Essay on Liberty." This delighted the boy, for it brought simplicity again
into matters which had seemed chaotic, and
provided a touchstone by which he could try
all Acts of Parliaments and all suggestions of
Reformers.   It was clear to him that Government had nothing to do with the poor, except
to secure their liberty as it secured that of
other citizens; he maintained in debate that
even workhouses were contrary to right reason,
though it might be inexpedient to level them
at one stroke to the ground ; he recommended
charity with all the approved safeguards to
his fellow members as a matter of private
enterprise.   It says much for Archie Rayner
that these fellow members liked him, in spite
of his long speeches; but then all his little
world liked him.   If he, who had not yet

learned the meaning of Philosophy, philosophized at too great length, he philosophized
without effeminacy; for he loved the river
in summer and the foot-ball field in winter,
and, like the Athenians, he did much of his
living, and even some of his debating, in
fairest places and in the happy outer air.

When Archie went up to Oxford, he
thought that he knew a great deal about
many things, and he was confident at least
that he carried with him the right foundation
of the right political faith. He turned
eagerly to the other Freshmen to see what
their views were; and, since he had gone up
to an eminently intellectual College, he found
no lack of opinions. He may be said to have
run straight into the arms of a young
Mazzinist, and within twenty-four hours his
radicalism had lost what now seemed to him
its insular character; his zeal for Liberty had
extended as far as the Sclavs, of whose
existence he had been previously unaware;
and his dry political maxims had been flooded

by a new enthusiasm and glorified by all the
sacred emotions of religion. With this
young Mazzinist, Thomas Beck, who had
been the prize boy of a great town in the
North, and who was supported at Oxford by
contributions of his wealthier townsfolk,
Archie Rayner struck up a warm friendship.
With him and with other youths he ex-
changed ideas, as if ideas were inexhaustible.
It was a splendid time; but not much of it
was exhausted before all their little opinions,
which had seemed to be so firmly based,
were crumbling. They discussed everything;
nothing was to be accepted without discussion; and the result was that Beck began
to admit that Mazzini had expected too
much from average people, and that men
were hungry and wicked even in Republics;
while Archie was delighted with his new
talent for paradox, and began to make light
of that Liberty which included the liberty to
be drunk daily, to starve in peace, and to
spread disease by the foul condition of the

house, which was, as freemen loved to say, an Englishman's castle.

These happy and inquiring young men devoured the volumes of Carlyle, and attended in due course lectures on Philosophy. From Carlyle and from the metaphysicians, as from their own growth and from their own discussions, they learned that the universe was yet deeper and higher than they had thought, more mysterious, more complicated. It was no longer so simple a matter for a young man to decide what he should do with his life. To this practical question Archie Rayner, who was at bottom a very practical person, was for ever returning, to the vexation of some of his more brilliant comrades, who preferred wider and less personal considerations. The universe alone was wide enough for them; but Archie stuck firmly to his intention of being of some use in the world. Only it had become hard for him to tell how he could be of most use, or indeed of any use at all. From Carlyle, for example,

he learned that he should do that work which
lay nearest to his hands : but this was small
help to Archie, who declared with conviction
that he could see no work close to his hands.
He was an only child ; he had enough money ;
he objected to be rich.   Since he could not
believe that it was his duty to make money,
he could see no reason for embracing any one
of the obvious professions.   He regarded
lawyers as a necessary evil ; his success at
the Bar would take work from men who
needed it more, and who would serve the
public at least as well.   He did not wish to
compete with his mother in spinning delicate
sentences ; he had at that time an amused
contempt for novels.   He might take a good
degree and might get a Fellowship ; but the
idea of eternal Oxford did not please him ; it
seemed like the prolonging of youth without
remaining young.   He was not a poet.
Finally, he could not give his life to the
service of the poor, for he did not know how
best to serve them.   His beliefs had got loose ;

his opinions were changing under each new influence which he met; he was but twenty-three years old. When he had taken his degree with credit, the only fact, of which he felt certain, was that it would be well for him to go away alone for a while and to consider in solitude that same old question, what work he should do in the world. So he made up his mind to go straight from Balliol to the Rocky Mountains, and for all his solemn doubts he felt a boyish joy in the contrast. His mother shed some natural tears: she dreamed of bears and of Indians, and woke sobbing. She would rather have seen him safe in studious chambers, or, and this would have been best of all, in some such delightful vicarage as she had described in more than one of her novels. But he was determined to go, and, though he was very kind to his mother, he went.

Archie had gone to think among the mountains. He found a silent mate, who knew them well, and he and his new friend camped out together. The eternal snow, the cañons cut deep in the mountains as if with one stroke of a knife of preternatural sharpness, above all the keen pure air, delighted the boy. Perhaps he thought; it is certain that he walked long distances in search of black-tailed deer, and was less eager for a time to decide upon a life's career than to attain to a high degree of accuracy with the rifle. He once saw a bear and missed him clean, and the depression, from which he suffered for the next twenty-four hours, brought back on him in a flood his doubts of the nature of the universe and of his mission therein. But he could not be down-hearted in that delightful air; his breath quickened, his ears tingled, and he seemed within a little of flying; at night he lay in his blankets reading Schwegler's " History of Philosophy," while his comrade smoked in silence. Whether this life would have led the boy to a definite decision about his future, it is impossible to say ; for it was cut short, before its first charm had begun to

fail, by the most amazing news. One day
he had been forced to journey down to
Colorado Springs for a few necessaries of life,
and he found there some letters, which told
him that he had become Lord Lorrilaire, and
had acquired, as heir of the late lord, lands
and houses and a great fortune in money.

Archie had not completed his University
education without being asked if he were one
of the Rayners of Langley ; he had answered
generally that he believed so, and, if in his
most communicative mood, he had added the
information that the Rayners of Langley had
done very well without him. Indeed, the
late Lord Lorrilaire, who was the head of the
family, had never shown that he was aware
that there was a widowed Mrs. Rayner, who
was connected with his family. The title
and estates had gone from father to son for
many generations ; and it had not occurred to
this particular father that there was any
doubt that the title and estates would pass in
due course from him to his son. He was by

no means an old man, and his son was strong and active and sure to marry soon, as was the plain duty of an only son. Now, it happened that Lord Lorrilaire paid a visit to the house of a friend, and that this house, though it combined great dignity and antiquity with all the modern luxuries, was in a state by no means satisfactory to sanitary inspectors. Lord Lorrilaire carried home from this visit the seeds of typhoid fever ; he was stout and ruddy and too much inclined to fever ; it was presently known that he was in great danger. They telegraphed to his son, who was travelling in India ; and on the next day they were forced to telegraph again that Lord Lorrilaire was dead. The second telegram crossed another sent from India, which brought news that his son had had an accident while riding through a river and had been drowned, before help could be given. It was a question, which interested Society at the moment, whether the father or the son had died first. A question, which interested them more, was the question, who was the heir; but the people best informed were at a loss. Even Lady Jane Lock did not know, nor could she find the right man in the Peerage. It was reserved for the family lawyers, not without a moment's doubt, to declare that the title and estates in Limeshire, Loamshire, and the Parish of St. Mary-la-Bonne, passed to Archibald, only son of the late Captain Rayner of the Royal Artillery. Thus Archie had become a lord. He blushed in Colorado Springs as he learned it. He felt a fool; that was his first feeling. He rode back to camp, and blushed again as he told his mate. "How's that?" said the mate, who had come West from Chicago.— "What in thunder are you?"

"I'm a lord," said Archie; "and I've got to go home and learn the business."

He presented the History of Philosophy to his friend, and would have given him the rifle too, had he not been so quietly confident of the superiority of American weapons. He felt that he could give away things with an easy hand; that was one advantage any way. He said good-bye to his mate and to the mountains, which he loved; went down to Pueblo and took the train; and he did not rest from travelling till he reached London.

It is not surprising that Archie Rayner was confused by this strange stroke of fortune. Before he was sure of his own religion, he found that he had Church-livings to give away. Discontented with both the parties, which monopolized the field of politics, he was placed in a position, which had always been one of great political influence. Ignorant of society, and especially of women, he was received by society with a simple friendliness, and with a frank curiosity which was hardly impertinent. On the whole he enjoyed himself immensely, almost as much as in his first days in the Rockies. And he began to wonder if his practical question were not answered. Family lawyers, men of the world, charming women, seemed all to agree that his course in life was clear. Nobody even asked him what he meant to do. Certainly now there was work to his hand, if he chose to do it. To do the work nearest to him was perhaps the best answer, which he had got to all his old questioning. There were clear duties attached to this new position of his; this ought to content him. What if he should let himself go and see what would happen to him? It was easy; it would be great fun. If he found himself a prop of the Conservative party, was it not perhaps the party of the most real and practical reforms? If he found himself in love, that might be delightful. Heretofore he had been in love with phantoms. Now these young girls in society were charming, with their little airs and fashions, and their belief that they knew the world; and there was not one of them handsomer or more interesting than Elizabeth Lock. In her he fancied that there was something deeper than in the others; and certainly her hair was of the most beautiful colour. So he had let himself drift through a London season and had gone down safe to his mother in her quiet home. And then the time had come, when his uncle Sir Villiers Hickory, and his aunt Mrs. Dormer (for his mother was dismayed at the idea of leaving her own studio and her own neighbourhood), had decreed that he must entertain a party, a very little one for a beginning, at Langley Castle. Thither he went as to a comedy, and laughed when he thought that the chief player would be himself. Perhaps he was but a dancing doll, and others would pull the strings; but even that thought made him laugh. He had let himself go for a while; he could always pull up when he liked; he was sure of that. So partly by train and partly on foot the heir had come to his own, and now lay asleep under the imposing roof of Langley Castle, drawing his breath with happiness, and yet, it seems, in truly parlous state.

CHAPTER IV.

"I AM the most unlucky devil in the world," said Leonard Vale. If he were unlucky, he did not seem to be uncomfortable. He was in the pleasant morning-room of Langley Castle; he had pulled the biggest arm-chair near to the fire, and he almost lay in it with his long legs stretched far on to the rug before him. His long white hands, each weighted with a single heavy ring, lay limp along the arms of the chair; his great dark eyes were half closed, as if it were too much trouble to raise the lids; he seemed to be speaking to his long, slender feet.

Mrs. Chauncey, who was the only other person in the room, made no comment on the speech of the young man. She had heard it before. Indeed, in the early hours of the

day Leonard Vale was apt to take this view
of himself, and to mention it to anybody to
whom he spoke at all ; and Clara Chauncey,
who was an old friend, paid no more attention
to his speeches of this sort, if spoken before
luncheon, than she would have paid to the
natural expressions of a sleepy cat.   However, she was inclined at the moment to talk.
She too had made herself comfortable in a
feminine fashion.   For a woman, who is well
dressed for the day, there is no comfort in a
large arm-chair.   She had seated herself in
an armless chair with a convenient back, and
placed her feet, which were two of her best
points, on a puffy footstool.   Her eyes were
not half closed.   On the contrary, they were
wide open, and they regarded the young man
opposite with that innocent inquiring gaze
which Mrs. Chauncey used often and often
with effect.   She would have laughed at the
idea that she wished to produce an effect on
this youth, whom she chose to regard as a boy
and as a fit object for lectures ; but these

little arts of charming women naturally become habits in time, so that it is no rare thing to see an habitually fascinating lady making eyes at her housekeeper, while her mind is wholly busy with the important question of the day's dinner.

"My dear boy," said Mrs. Chauncey, fixing her round candid eyes upon Leonard, "you smoke too many cigarettes. That's what's the matter with you."

"I like that from you," he said without moving or turning his eyes.

"Oh, I have given up smoking," she said, feeling a keener interest in the talk as it turned on herself.

"Since when?"

"Since so many women took to it," she said; "it is commonplace now. Lady J. smokes; her maid told mine; she says it is for asthma; it is so droll to have a reason." All this she said with her pretty surprised air. Pretty she still was beyond all question, although she was always telling people with

her delightful simplicity that she was no
longer young. It is true that her face was
now pale and a little too thin, but the brown
eyes were all the more effective. " Ah, you
boys ! " she said again after a minute ; " you
do ask so much of life. Look at me." He
turned a lack-lustre eye upon her, as she continued. " Suppose I were to begin complaining. What a tale I could tell ! Married
to a—to my husband, to a man who cared for
nothing but yachting, I who couldn't go on a
river without qualms ! " He began to laugh
in spite of himself. She regarded him
gravely ; her talk was like the artless prattle
of a child. " All on account of that yachting,
and because I really could not spend my life
at all sorts of angles, I have been cruelly
abused and talked about, and——"

" You don't mind that much."

" That shows how much you know. I
used to think that I didn't mind what women
said ; I was very foolish and defiant ; I know
a great deal better now." She emitted a

little sigh. He could not help showing that
he was a little amused; he thought her the
cleverest woman in the world. She needed
very little encouragement to induce her to
continue to talk about herself.

"I lost the privilege," she said gravely, "of
going to many of the dullest country houses
in England." He laughed. "You need not
laugh," she said; "all my energies, my whole
being is now directed to the one purpose of
creeping back."

"Of what?"

"Of creeping back into those houses. Dear
Susan Dormer! She has never turned her
back, her broad back, upon me. I cannot
tell you how full of peace and gratitude I feel
now when I am staying at Langley. Did you
see the little paragraph in the paper?"

"I can't say I did."

"'Mrs. Chauncey has left town for Langley
Castle,'" she murmured; "how peaceful it
sounds, and how prosperous! The one
thing," she continued presently, "which all

women find absolutely necessary is to be able to look down on some other women. I am assured that you find that among the very lowest. I am now able to look down on women who do not stay at Langley."

"You will be able to look down on me pretty soon," he said, relapsing into sullenness.

"My dear boy," she said, "I always have looked down upon you; but you are not a woman, if you are a little womanish."

"You needn't abuse me; I am down enough on my luck, heaven knows!"

"Does it?" she asked with her innocent gravity. "What is the matter, if it is not cigarettes?"

He moved in his chair and grumbled inarticulately; at last with a voice full of injury he said—

"I used to come to you to help me."

"Ah, if it had been a bad habit, you wouldn't have given it up!"

"Oh, I don't suppose you'll care; I don't see why you should," he muttered.

"About what?" she asked.

"About my getting the sack."

"The sack! What for?" she asked again.

"You ain't generally so stupid, Clara; you must know that these women are going to marry Archie."

"Are you so fond of your cousin Archie," she asked after a minute, "that you cannot bear the idea of his belonging to another?"

"Well," he answered defiantly, "it is uncommon hard on him; he hasn't had a bit of fun; and it's deuced hard on *me*. Here am I, older than him, and quite as near to the late lord, only it happened to be through a woman instead of a man."

"Ah, that makes a difference," she said; "women don't count; they never do."

"Well, it does seem hard lines," he said, aroused to a perceptibly higher level of animation, "that he should have every blessed thing which a man can want, and that I, who used to come here all the time and make myself useful——"

" Useful ? " she asked with an air of surprise ;
" my dear boy !   Useful ? "

" Well, it is deuced hard.   He was never
near the place in his life till he came to take
possession."

" But why the sack ? " she asked.   " I
thought that he had done the handsome thing
by you.   I hear that you've taken the best
rooms in the house for yourself."

" Who told you that ? "

" My maid.   She had it from your man."

" Well, I really shouldn't go listening to
the servants' gossip," he said sulkily.

" Wouldn't you ?   You are so wrong.   I
always do.   I learn everything from my maid.
It is such a good plan ; it amuses her so much
that she doesn't bother about her wages ; she
is like a friend, you know ; she adores me."

As he made no comment on these frank
statements, she continued—

" My maid says that you have taken the
whole Tower wing for yourself and made it
charming."

"It's only three rooms," he said; "and nobody used them. They were given up to mouldy targets and broken bird-cages—and black-beetles, I dare say."

"Ugh!" she said with a shudder.

"I thought I was more worthy than a black-beetle. Perhaps I flattered myself." He said this with more pleasure, feeling as if he too could be witty.

"Perhaps," she said with gravity; "one never knows. And you have done the rooms well?"

"I think I've made 'em nice," he answered comfortably. "Archie told me to do what I liked with them, you know."

"And to send the bill to him," she said, as if completing his sentence.

"It wouldn't be much good their sending it to me," he said. "Of course he felt that I'd been devilishly badly treated—oh, I don't complain of Archie."

"Don't you? But you don't want him to be married and to live happy ever after; and you do want to stay in your nice rooms, curled up like a gorged fox in a rabbit-warren."

" You needn't call names," he muttered.

" My dear boy," she said, " you are quite right: of course you want to stay where you are, and to drink his wine and to shoot his coverts and to ride his horses——"

" When I'm not too jumpy," he said, as she paused at a loss for the next luxury. " You know all about me, Clara," he continued ; " I always told you everything. You know I'm a nervous subject; and you know I can't do without the luxuries of life. How can I?"

" Nerves and luxuries," she remarked thoughtfully, as if to herself. " How can I help you?" she asked him presently.

" You might advise me."

" You don't want me to flirt with the boy," she said slowly, looking at him gravely with her round artless eyes ; " I am old enough to be his mother."

" Clara, what nonsense——" he began.

"It can't be done," she said; "you forget
that I am creeping back. It might have
amused me once, just to cut out the girl, and
no harm done; but now—my dear boy, *I*
should get the sack: I would much rather it
was you who got the sack."

"Thank you!"

"I am just trembling in the balance with
Lady J. now," she said; "I am truckling to
her, grovelling; she was dreadfully annoyed
at finding me here; she wanted Susan
Dormer to give me warning on the spot.
Expect nothing from me. I have no energies
left except for creeping back."

Leonard Vale did not expostulate with his
friend. He only shifted himself a little in
his chair, pulled his sleek black moustache
into a point, and bit his under lip. Mrs.
Chauncey knew in a moment that he had not
yet said what he wished to say, and that she
had been wrong in thinking that he wished
her to divert young Lord Lorrilaire from the
dangers of matrimony.

"There's somebody else, you know," he said at last, "who might save Archie—I wanted to ask your advice, you know—if she were to come down, you know—— "

"Who?"

"You see, she's the only woman in London who knew Archie before. She was the parson's daughter down at his home, wherever it was."

A slight change of expression came into Mrs. Chauncey's eyes, and the thin sensitive lips, which had been so long schooled in the concealment of feeling, pressed each other a little more tightly. She knew well of whom he was speaking, but she chose to keep her look of inquiry.

"It's Mrs. Rutherford," he said, still looking at his boots. Then, as her continued silence made him nervous, he gave one glance in her direction, looked away again, and went on speaking.

"You see, she don't want Archie to marry yet; she thinks he don't know anything of the world, and that she knows all about it; she thinks she's his only friend and has got a sort of mission to save him from match-making mothers; she was furious with Lady J. in London."

"She is very pretty," said Mrs. Chauncey.

"I wish you'd advise me," he said; "I wish you'd tell me if it would do for her to come down here."

"You have asked her to come already," she said quietly.

He opened his mouth as if he were going to lie, but he shut it again and pulled himself into a more upright position. "It's no good trying to humbug you," he said: "I've not asked her, for I've no right to ask anybody; but I have written to her and told her who are here."

"And that will bring her without com-mitting you to anything."

"Do you think she'll come?" he asked almost deferentially.

"You ought to know best," she said frankly; "she certainly is very pretty."

"What's that got to do with it?"

Clara Chauncey knew that she was vexed, and did not mean to show it. It has been said that there is no love without jealousy: however that may be, there is plenty of jealousy without love. She was jealous now. She knew perfectly well that this boy was trying to break to her diplomatically that a younger and prettier woman was coming, and that he thought it necessary to be diplomatic because he thought that she would be jealous of his devotion to the new-comer. She would have liked to impress upon him with something more convincing than words, with the fire-irons perhaps, how very little she cared or ever had cared about him. But, though it is perfectly true that her warmest feeling for Leonard had been a mild amusement in forming, as she called it, a handsome boy, who came to tea and could be sent for theatre tickets, yet it is no less true that it annoyed her to think of his devoting himself to anybody else. It annoyed her that she

would no longer be the pretty married woman
of the party; it annoyed her that this other
woman was so young and looked so happy;
it annoyed her most of all that this sulky
youth was trying to manage her and thought
that she would be jealous on his account.
His side-long looks annoyed her.

"Of course she will come," she said : " she
will propose herself to Lord Lorrilaire; she
will think it great fun to invite herself. She
is an absurd little creature, married out of a
parson's schoolroom, and thinks she knows
the world; but it is a pretty absurdity. She
will come down full of importance to save
the friend of her childhood. You admire her
very much, don't you?" She asked this
with a delightful frankness and one of her
rare smiles.

"Oh, of course I admire Mrs. Tom," he said
with a clumsy masculine effort to answer her
in the same tone; "everybody admired her;
it was the thing this year."

"And I do not wonder," she said ; "she is

so pretty and so fresh, so refreshingly fresh. It will be very pleasant for you if she comes."

"It will save my place for me," he said with a happy inspiration; "that's what matters to me."

She sat looking at him with her air of quiet study. "Yes," she said, "that is what will always matter most to you. Of course it is too late to stop this plot of yours."

"There's no plot of mine," he said; "I just told her who were here. If she likes to propose herself, it's her own look-out."

"If she gets into a scrape," she said, "that is her own look-out too. She need not look to you to help her." She made these statements with the coolness and certainty of a mathematical professor; and they stung Leonard Vale to some show of temper.

"Upon my word, Clara," he said, "you seem to be trying to say the most disagreeable things you can."

"Who? I?" She seemed to be truly surprised.

"Yes, you," he answered; "but never mind! I'm so down that any one may hit me—and you most of all, of course." He slipped back to his depressed and dependent air.

"Of course," she said, "you told me nothing of this until it was too late to stop her coming."

"Oh, I dare say you can stop it, if you like," he said, "and leave poor Archie to be married, and set me adrift again just when I have a chance of pulling up and staying quiet and paying my debts—— "

"And living on your rich bachelor cousin," she added for him, as he paused. "And the husband?" she asked presently; "has Mr. Rutherford no say in the matter?"

"Not much," answered Leonard, with a short laugh.

"Really?" she said; "I used to know him a little. I should not have thought that he was that sort of man."

"She'll come, if she likes," said he, nodding his head.

His knowing air exasperated Mrs. Chauncey. She had a great power of self-control, but she knew that, if she continued to sit opposite to Leonard, she would presently say more than she meant to, show her annoyance, and then, angry with herself for showing annoyance, say yet more, and finally have several rash speeches of which to repent at leisure. So she rose from her chair, and looked at the clock, and said, " I cannot waste any more of my morning in talking to you; " and so walked out of the room.

Leonard Vale, left alone, let himself slide even lower down in his low arm-chair, and pushed his hands deep down into his trousers' pockets. He felt ill-used by fortune and by friends; he doubted if he had any friends. He could not tell if this Clara Chauncey, who had pretended to be his friend and to lecture him for his good, meant to help him or to hinder him at this crisis. He told himself that after such a series of bad things, as only an unlucky chap experiences, he had at last

come in for a good thing; and that now it
was at least ten to one that he would lose it.
He recalled his first annoyance when he
found that he was not to be a penny the
better for the death of the late lord, and his
amazement when the present man, fresh from
Colorado, had burst in upon him in his
lodgings, sympathized warmly with his sense
of ill-usage, and asked as a matter of course
to be allowed to pay his debts, and to set him
on his legs again. Since that astonishing
visit Lenny had been wondering at odd times
what this prosperous cousin (for Archie had
insisted on the cousinship, which was none of
the nearest) expected to get out of him in
return. He had made a half-hearted sugges-
tion that he should be an agent or sub-agent
or something, but Archie had received it as a
joke. He had a great many acquaintances
whom it was considered a treat to know,
male and female, of all shades ; but his cousin
did not seem even to wish for introductions.
He knew a man, who was one of the few men

who knew a horse; but his cousin had
already commissioned his uncle Sir Villiers
to fill his stables.   He knew the correct place
to go to for cigarettes and the champagne
which it was right to drink that year; and
Archie received his information on these
points, but rather as if he humoured him.

Lenny, recumbent in the big arm-chair,
wondered once more if this new Lord
Lorrilaire could be such a flat as to have paid
his debts and filled his pockets for nothing.
He could not believe that anybody would
encumber himself unasked and at the very
start of his life with poor relations.   He
assured himself with a knowing nod that if
he had come in for all this, he would have
had no hangers-on.   If he did not imagine
himself kicking himself out of Langley Castle,
it was only because his imagination was
limited.   Nevertheless, he felt that he would
be injured more deeply than ever, if he were
made to lose his hold now.   And this hang-
ing-on was so uncertain a business for any

one who was not quite a prehensile ape.
Before luncheon and in his dejected mood he
was half inclined to give the whole thing up.
The difficulties seemed enormous; he felt
chilly, in spite of the good fire, as he thought
of all the trouble; he would have to walk
among egg-shells. He had seen the suspicion
of him in the eyes of Lady Jane Lock within
half an hour of her arrival. Mrs. Dormer
was always kind, and Sir Villiers had been a
friend of his father; but Sir Villiers had a
keen eye, and Mrs. Dormer saw so much more
than she seemed to. And then his thoughts
passed again to Clara Chauncey, and stirred
him to fresh annoyance. Why in the world
could not she say if she would help him or
not? If not, he might as well be packing
his portmanteau. And Dora Rutherford?
Would she come? If she came, would it be
known that he had brought her? He hoped
that she would come, and yet he feared. He
feared his very hope, for it surprised him by
his strength. If he could not trust his

friends, he could not trust himself either. He knew that his nerves might fail him at any time ; he dared not answer for his self-control at a critical moment. Already he felt feverish and good for nothing. Again he pronounced himself, with something like a smothered howl, to be the most unlucky brute in the world.

CHAPTER V.

YOUNG Lord Lorrilaire was grumbling too, as he got himself into his clothes with unusual difficulty on the morning after his return to Langleydale. He had plunged into his country-house party, and risen to the surface again and felt the better. And then the rest of his day had been full of amusing discoveries, which had made it almost as fascinating as a young adventurer's first day in a new world. And yet he grumbled, as he dressed himself. He did not like to spend so much time in the adornment of his person; it seemed absurd; and yet for that day at least he was bound to be particular about each wrinkle, and each button. He had grown so warm while he strove so conscientiously for accuracy, that

he had opened his windows to their utmost
width, and the room, in which he still felt a
stranger and explorer, was full of the clear
cool air.   A little too clear and cool it was
for the ideal hunting morning; but to Archie
it seemed that on that portentous day the
hunting was of small importance.   He was
to display himself, as his uncle had arranged,
to the members of the Hunt ; he felt as if he
were the object of the chase, and as if land-
lords, farmers, the town contingent from
Langstone, even horses and hounds were
coming out to find him instead of the fox.
His hat, his tie, his spurs, every detail of his
appearance would be criticized, and his seat
and his hands, about which no one had cared
in happy days gone by.   Severe eyes would
be on his back as he rode at a hedge, mark
him if he deviated from a rigid line across
country, betray amazement if he grew bored
and went home.   Of his clothes he felt confident, for he had gone to him, whom Lenny
had described tersely as the only breeches-

maker; but this putting them on was a tiresome business. It was only better than yielding himself to the hand of his bodyservant; for he had not had a body-servant since he had grown too big for a nurse, and he never breathed freely now till he had dismissed this most oppressive burden of his state. He would much rather help his valet into his clothes than be helped into his own.

As Archie tugged and buttoned, he remembered other days, some at Oxford, and some in his mother's neighbourhood at home, when after duly counting the cost he had treated himself to a day's hunting. Much fun he had enjoyed upon hardly-worked strange-looking beasts, and, as they were always ready to go and his treats in this kind were rare, he had ridden his hardest and seen what he could. Much fun he had enjoyed; and now memory, as is her happy way, smoothed away the little mishaps and discomforts, the unexpected cropper and the long ride home upon a tired screw, and showed him the pleasure only. Nobody cared then what he wore, or how he rode ; he did not feel as if he were clad in pasteboard, and he rode to please himself. Now it seemed to him that he must ride to satisfy his neighbours ; his uncle was evidently anxious, lest he should not show off the horses, which he had chosen. Archie thought of that row of animals in prime condition, and imagined each one of them expecting to be taken out in turn. It seemed as if it would take all his life, be the life's business of which he had dreamed, a business as distinct from pleasure as any other business, a truly British amusement solemn as affairs of State, affording occupation to the unemployed, and with as little to show for it in the end as the exercise of the treadmill. Having arrived at this thought, he began to smile again, partly because he was nearly dressed, partly because the thought itself was extravagant. After all, he would presently feel a good horse moving under him, and that was pleasure ;

and, if the neighbours were critical, it was
probably an exaggeration to assert that they
would value him more than the fox; the fox,
though probably he was better known in the
county, would after all excite the keener
interest. He began to smile at his own folly
in taking himself as seriously as if he were
an Under-Secretary, or the manager of a
theatre. And the air kept coming in at the
open window, bringing health and good
spirits, if it were by a touch too keen to
satisfy the exigent sportsman; and presently,
when his glass showed him a cheerful young
Englishman blushing at his own splendour,
he even felt a slight pleasure in being
properly turned out for the first time in his
life. He restrained a tendency to fright his
castle from its tremendous propriety with a
" view halloa ! " and descended happy, if stiff,
to meet his guests at breakfast.

In dangerously easy mood was young
Lord Lorrilaire, as he descended the staircase
somewhat stiffly in his admirable breeches.

It even seemed the best fun possible to let things slide, and himself slide with them. It was likely that all things, his very life itself, would be settled for him, before he had done saying to himself that there was time to spare, and that he could assert himself on any future day. In the mean time it was pleasant and easy to please everybody.

Lady Jane Lock did not approve of girls going out hunting. It was opposed to her theories of female education; and the success of her daughters so far had given her no cause to doubt the wisdom of her theories. But she knew that Elizabeth was different; she was not quite sure that she understood Elizabeth, though it seemed monstrous that she should not understand her own child. Elizabeth was never so happy as when she was on a horse; and, when she longed for a day's hunting and an absolutely fit and proper guardian was at hand, her mother did not always prevent her. She did not prevent her on this day. She had asked her usual

questions on the previous evening, and had
been assured that it was an easy sociable
country with convenient gates and lanes, and
further, that the meet was not one of the
best. So she had entrusted her precious
child to Sir Villiers, who was the most
trustworthy of pioneers; and she contented
herself by making her usual statement that
Elizabeth did not hunt, and so sent her out
hunting.

The meet was so near that they all mounted
their hunters at the door; and Archie
observed with a smile that after all a good
many of his new possessions would be ex-
ercised on that day. He was mounting Sir
Villiers of course, and Lenny, and the best
and kindest of the lot was brought round
with a side-saddle for Miss Lock. And
there was Tony Fotheringham, too, who
completed this country-house party. Tony
was one of Archie's new friends, and one who
amused him always by a seriousness, which
seemed highly comical in one so young and

so rosy. Tony was two years younger than his host, and was as smooth and ruddy as the advertisement of a patent food; but he took great care of himself and gave a great deal of thought to his health. Even now, as he sat on a horse which seemed distinctly too big for him, he looked seriously at the dining-room window, through which Mrs. Dormer was gazing at the group, and was inclined to repent that he had not remained at home and had a good long talk with that sympathetic lady about his symptoms. However, it was too late for repentance, and he rode away with the rest, while Lady Jane stood on a step, defiant of the crisp air, and watched her girl and approved the fit of her habit. The girl was riding with Sir Villiers, as she ought; but her mother thought that she need not have talked so eagerly to him that it was as good as a hint to Lord Lorrilaire not to interrupt the conversation. She said to herself with some vexation that it was just like Elizabeth, whose notorious fault was

want of animation, to be animated at the
wrong moment; but then a day's hunting
was always becoming to Elizabeth and gave
her a colour and made her eyes sparkle. So
after all this might be a most fortunate day.
Lady Jane watched them, till they had ridden
out of sight, with her usual desire to re-
arrange them and to order them all to do her
will, but not without good hope. She did not
spare a single thought for Bolitho.

Archie's spirits rose with the movements
of his horse, and they did not even fall when
he was introduced to member after member
of the Hunt. These members were cordial
and brief; he forgot to think of their
criticisms; he began to feel the old ardour of
the chase. Nor did his pleasant spirits fail,
though the morning was spent in jogging
from covert to covert. It was pleasant to be
out on such a day, to receive friendly greet-
ings, to see hounds again after a long interval,
and to ride by the side of a handsome girl
who was flushed with excitement and the

eager hope of a run. And after luncheon
they did have a short run, and the country
was easy and pleasant, and both Archie and
Elizabeth went as well as anybody ; and,
when they pulled up, the girl turned on her
young host a face transfigured by new life
and light. Her red lips were parted, her
eyes were shining, and little wandering hairs
from her glossy head were curling above her
ears. As she leaned forward to caress the
neck of the good horse, she looked at his
owner with gratitude and triumph, and
Archie smiled back upon her with the
frankest admiration. Was he not happy
that he could give to this radiant being so
glorious a gallop ? There was some use in
wealth. The radiant being lost much of her
radiance when she found that there was to be
no more hunting on that day. She rebelled
promptly, and murmured against the Master,
who sent the hounds home so early. But she
recovered her temper and became happy
again, as they rode slowly homewards. She

discussed the run with Archie, who still rode
beside her; and when that subject was
exhausted, and soon, for after all it had been
a very short run, she went on talking with a
want of reserve which she never showed
except after excitement and quick exercise.
She had been expressing such love of the
country and its pleasures, that Archie reminded her that she had seemed very happy
sometimes in the London ball-rooms, which
she now held cheap.

"Oh yes," she said, "I liked this last
season; I hated my first season, but I liked
this; I began to know people, and I made
some friends, and I wasn't always thinking
if I was standing right or going into rooms
properly, and I didn't feel obliged to agree
with what everybody said to me."

Archie laughed.

"I shouldn't have thought that you would
ever have agreed with everybody," he said.

"But I did," she said emphatically, "and
I used to be ashamed of myself; I used to go

home and hate myself! But in my second season I didn't care, and, if I didn't agree with people, I said so, or I didn't answer and let them think me dull. That is what many people think me."

"Do they?" he asked; "they must be dull, I think; you are silent sometimes."

"What is the good of talking?" she asked.

"Well," he said, "it is supposed to convey ideas, when there are any. And what about your third season?"

"I shall like that better still," she answered. "You see, I don't care now what anybody says of me."

"Isn't that a trifle strong?" said Archie.

"No," she said. "I shall enjoy this next season," she continued after a minute, "as much as possible, and after that——"

She made so long a pause that he thought that she had forgotten that she had left her sentence unfinished. After all in these days no person of any pretension to fashion is expected to finish a sentence, and polite conversation is no more than an interchange of hints, generally about nothing. But Miss Lock had an unequivocal end for her sentence. "After that," she said, " I shall hate it."

Archie was much amused by her decision.

"Isn't it rather unnecessary," he asked, "to make up your mind so long before? You see you've a whole season before you, which you've decided to enjoy very much indeed; perhaps when that is over you will look forward to the next."

"No," she said with even more decision, and looking straight between her horse's ears. "No," she said; "I don't want to spend my life in going about to balls."

"It must be a bore," he said with prompt conviction; "I should hate it myself. What would you rather do?" He felt a real curiosity; it was a new idea to him that girls also could be tired of ball-going and such amusements. "What would you like to do ? " he asked.

"I don't know," she answered,—"hunt."

"Oh!" he said, disappointed; "but perhaps you would be tired of that after your three seasons; and besides, you can't do it in summer."

"Do you suppose that I don't know when people hunt?" she asked with scorn. Then, for they had turned into a road which had a nice broad border of grass, she touched her willing horse and set off at a canter. Archie followed her, and, when she had stopped and he was once more at her side, she said to him with superb unreasonableness, "Of course you think that no woman can care for anything but dancing and hunting."

"I thought it was you," he said, "who wanted to spend your life in hunting."

"Not at all," she said; "I should like to do something useful!"

"Useful?" he repeated. She nodded slightly, as if she did not care whether he believed her or not. She had certainly surprised him. He had held it most natural that a boy, whose ideas were not wholly confined to horses, should wish to be useful in the world; but that a girl, and a fashionable girl, should have such a wish, was a new fact for him. He had seen little of such girls and thought little about them. Was this a fact at all? He was not suspicious, but all the suspicion of which he was capable was ready to arise in him when he considered girls. He knew his ignorance of them; and he wondered now if this girl who, under the influence of excitement and the healthy day, was really beautiful, had any real desire of anything but amusement; he supposed that girls practised the art of being agreeable, and he wondered if this girl were assuming a more serious view that she might please him, who had been ticketed without doubt by her world as a prig. She looked beautiful; he dismissed his uneasy doubt, as he looked at her. Moreover he asked himself why he should trouble himself, if she did care to pose a little for his benefit?

"Well?" she asked, since he kept silence;

"you think that's humbug, I suppose? I suppose that you think that no woman can do any good? Delia, my sister—she married a parson—a clergyman, I mean—I promised not to call him a parson."

"Is that what you mean?" he asked, laughing. "Do you mean that you would marry a pars—clergyman, I mean?"

"No."

"Why not? Oh, I beg your pardon if I am asking too many questions."

"I don't mind," she said. "I am not good enough; that's why."

"As good as lots of parsons," he responded quickly—"well, clergymen, then."

"Why do you talk as if everybody ought to marry somebody?" she asked.

"Isn't it the best thing for most people?" he asked in his turn.

."I don't pretend to know," she said. She gave a little laugh, which had a touch of malice in it. "It's a bad look out," she said, "if it is so; our men friends don't marry—they can't afford it, or it's not the thing. Ask Mr. Fotheringham."

" Tony ! " called out Lord Lorrilaire, turning in his saddle. Everybody called him " Tony," though there seemed to be no better reason than that his name was " Francis Algernon." Tony rode up to them. He was glad to join them, for he had been jogging in the rear with Leonard Vale, who had been the most gloomy of companions. Leonard had been looking at the backs of his cousin and the young lady, and had fallen into deep despondency, declaring to himself that all was over, and that his days in Langleydale were numbered. Perhaps he would never again ride this beast, which suited him so well ; and at this thought he jerked the mouth of the beast which suited him so well and gave him the spur. He was apt to hurt the nearest creature, which felt, when he was annoyed. From this and other signs Tony had gathered that Lenny was out of temper ; and so he left him without regret, and joined the pair in front. "Is it true," asked Archie, "that men don't marry nowadays?"

Tony considered the question with due gravity. It was even repeated before he answered it. "Well," he asked then, "what can a chap do? What with huntin' and goin' racin' it's hard enough to live now anyway! Most chaps are stone-broke without marryin'."

"What did I tell you?" asked Miss Lock of Archie. "Mr. Tony knows. He knows everything."

"Not quite," said Tony, regarding her in the evening light with frank admiration. He often declared that Elizabeth Lock was "about as handsome as they make 'em." "The nicest chaps can't afford to marry," he said, beaming amiably upon her.

"How sad!" she answered. "What a pity that only poor men are nice!" So saying, she cantered suddenly forward away from the young men, who began to jog on in pursuit side by side.

"I say," said Tony, when he had been for

some time in deep thought, "wasn't that rather a nasty one for you ? "

" What ? " asked Archie.

" That about only poor men being nice."

Archie only laughed ; and then Tony laughed too, and cried out " Good old Archie ! " which was one of his favourite phrases, kindly and encouraging, and coming in well at almost all times.

CHAPTER VI.

In the mean time, while her daughter was riding in the happy air, Lady Jane Lock was in full enjoyment at home of that flattering excitement which immediately precedes complete success, and is even more delightful. She had written her morning's letters; she had eaten her substantial luncheon; and, when she returned from her afternoon's walk (she was a great believer in "the constitutional"), she was in a fine glow of virtue. She had taken as her companion by the way Tony Fotheringham's umbrella, which its careful owner never allowed to touch the ground, and with this for her walking-stick she had stumped valiantly through the lanes, which after the slight frost of the night had been growing softer all day long under the

genial influences of sun and thaw. She had
left in the hall the precious umbrella with its
ferule muddy, battered, and knocked to one side
like the hat of a drunken man ; but she still
wore her plain felt hat and her braided black
jacket, as she stood with her straight back to
the cheerful fire with the air of a man, if not
of a field-marshal. However it may be with a
commander in the field, it is certain that almost
every woman, when the fortunes of the day
incline distinctly to her side, while yet enough
of doubt remains to feed the excitement of her
spirit, finds it hard to keep silence. Policy
may still prevent her from announcing her
game and prematurely singing her song of
victory ; but her choice of subjects will indicate
the direction of her thoughts, and it will be
hard for her to keep out of her voice the
sound of exultation. Lady Jane knew that
the tea, for which she had conscientiously
prepared herself by solitary exercise, would
soon be there, and that the young people
would soon be back from hunting ; and in the

mean time she could relieve herself by making a few general remarks. It was a good time for talk, for it was growing too dark for reading, and the lights had not yet been brought in. Mrs. Dormer had put down her novel with a tiny comical yawn; and Mrs. Chauncey, for her part, was ready at this time to give the most complimentary attention to all the observations of Lady Jane Lock.

"What I have always said to my girls," said Lady Jane, "is this. When you marry, make up your mind to have a house that people care to come to. It isn't the size of the house or the place; it's the people you meet there; that's what people care about."

"How true!" pronounced Clara Chauncey, from the shadows among which she sat.

"If you mean to have the right sort of house," continued Lady Jane, "you must be firm at first. That is what I tell my girls. There is no sense in choking up your houses with a lot of dull people just because they happen to be old friends of the family, or because your aunt Deborah married their uncle What's-his-name. There's no sense in it; and, if you do it, you never will get the right people to come to stay with you."

"How interesting!" murmured Mrs. Chauncey. "Cut off old friends and poor relations!"

"There is no need to be rude or disagreeable," said Lady Jane; "when you do meet these people about, you can always be *most* kind. It is a very nice trait to be just the same to people when you meet them, though you may not have met for years. Everybody says that."

"And it is so true," said Clara.

"When you do meet, be as affectionate and nice as possible, and ask after all their children and everything. Only be sure never to go to see them. If they *will* come to see you, never be at home. Some people let them in once and try to be so disagreeable that they won't come again; that is unlady-like and unnecessary. The simple thing is never to be at home, and never to return their calls."

"Admirable! You have such a talent for making things clear. But the husband's friends? Ain't they a difficulty?"

"Always be nice to your husband's friends," said Lady Jane promptly; "that is the very first thing which I tell my girls."

"But men do collect such strange friends," said Mrs. Chauncey; "I don't mean those whom they can't expect their wives to know; they present no difficulties whatever. I mean the friends who are respectable but impossible. What *do* you do with them?"

"Don't call," said Lady Jane; "that's all; it's just the same with them as with the others."

"But don't they make a fuss?—the husbands, I mean; husbands are so touchy."

"Yes," said Lady Jane; "they are touchy; but they are very forgetful. I tell my girls never to dispute with their husbands, always to seem to yield. If a man tells his wife to

call on the What's-his-names, she can put it
off, till he forgets all about it. He'll soon
forget all about it—or pretend to. I know
what men are. They like to have the right
people in their houses just as much as we
do; but they like us to do the unpleasant
part, and to pretend to know nothing about
it."

"Oh, Lady Jane," said Mrs. Chauncey, as if
she were in a sort of respectful ecstasy,
"what knowledge of the world—and of men!
They leave the dirty work to us, and look the
other way, and profit by it. That is the
whole duty of man."

"A husband is so easily managed," said
Lady Jane, "if you don't argue with him.
Of course he blusters. Some day he'll come
home and say that he has met his old friend
What's-his-name in the street, and can't
think what's the matter with him; he'll pretend to be annoyed with him and to wonder
why he never comes near him; but he will
know in his heart. All that you have got to

do is to smile sympathetically. Always meet
your husband with a smile! That is what
I tell my girls."

"Lucky girls!" murmured Mrs. Chauncey.
"Don't they say that to marry a Lock is a
liberal education? I am sure that I have
heard some such saying. When I look at a
place like this, and think of all the dangers,
to which rich young men are exposed, I am
tempted to say that there is no hope of safety
for them but in a well-trained wife."

"They don't know what is good for them,"
said Lady Jane, shortly.

"Oh, but they do," said Clara—"at least,
some of them do—don't they?" Her question
was so earnest and so innocent. "But then,"
she added, "they are so rare, these model
wives."

"Not at all," said Lady Jane; "there are
lots of nice well-brought-up English girls, if
the men would only look at them, instead of
going after Americans and things."

"Ah! but for a great position surely

something more is wanted—a something, a—— "

" Distinction," said Lady Jane, " the air noble—that is a matter of course."

" Or a matter of corsets," quickly said Mrs. Chauncey. Here Susan Dormer, who had been listening to the conversation with much placid enjoyment, began to shake with laughter, and Lady Jane, stung by the sudden idea that she was being trifled with, uttered a quick sound, which can only be described as a not unladylike snort.

"Oh, do forgive me!" cried Clara Chauncey ; " it is unpardonable, I know ; but really and truly it is often that, isn't it ? I have known such common dumpy women gain quite an air from really good stays. Nothing is more important."

To snort like the war-horse was in Lady Jane a sure sign of awakened suspicion, and it is by no means likely that she would have continued to express her views with so much freedom, even if the words " dumpy women "

had not been for her a new note of alarm.
She could not but know that she did not
stand much over five feet high, and that,
though she was very straight, active, and
energetic, she had acquired a certain solidity.
She had never approved of Mrs. Chauncey;
and it is likely that she already repented of
having favoured her with so many valuable
hints on the art of living. Whether she
would have contributed any further words
of wisdom will remain for ever uncertain;
for, with a pleasant sound of young voices
and some shutting of doors, the young people
came in from hunting, and brought a quite
new atmosphere into the fire-lit rooms. Archie
reported that Sir Villiers and Tony had gone
straight to the smoking-room, but that he
and Lenny wanted tea; and almost immediately tea was brought, and lamps so fully
shaded that they made mere small oases of
light in the soft warm dusk.

It was a pleasant hour, with fragrant tea
and chastened light, good rest after brisk

exercise, and liberal space. Perhaps nothing
is so expressive of luxury as the combination
of space and warmth. Even in most wintry
weather it is easy for the most modest of
men to make himself snug by shutting himself
up with a good fire in a tiny room; but a
large house brought to one warmth from
ground-floor to garret, whose inmates pass
without chill from lofty rooms to spacious
passages, is filled likewise with the very
atmosphere of prosperity. It was this atmosphere which Lady Jane Lock, who had
divested herself with an effort of the tight
jacket, breathed with satisfaction; and a sense
of mingled motherhood and ownership stole
over her active spirit, as her eyes looked from
the moderate room in which they sat, and saw
between the heavy *portières*, which had been
drawn widely open, the great, dimly lighted
space of handsome rooms beyond. The merest
fraction, more or less, of nose; the merest
shade, more or less, of natural yellow in the
hair; and all, of which this warm spacious-

ness was a sign, might be for one sister, while another was counting coal in a chilly vicarage.

Lady Jane Lock was in a mood of unusual softness, as she sipped her tea, when suddenly she seemed to hear a sound of wheels. It was very faint and far, but her alert spirit sprang, as it were, to arms. Nobody else seemed to hear anything; and she gave no sign, old campaigner as she was. She finished her tea and asked for a second cup: only her spirit was attentive. The front door was on the other side of the house, and at the further end. She could hear no more. She had just decided that her ears had played her false, or that some untimely tradesman's cart had come; she was just thinking that in the reign of a new mistress such irregularities of untimely tradesmen should not be, when she saw figures advancing through the obscurity of the farther room. The first figure was unmistakable, the rounded shape and noiseless amble of the butler; but who was following him? Lady Jane looked with a quick eye of inquiry at Mrs. Dormer, who had assured her unnecessarily often that no other guests were expected. Mrs. Dormer was looking too; and in a moment more the butler emerged into the less uncertain light and announced in his usual level tone—" Mrs. Rutherford."

She came in beaming, wrapped in handsome furs, bringing her own charm into the common place, as Venus leads her Graces. Her bright colour was the brighter for the evening cold; her eyes were sparkling; and even under the weight of fur her tall, slender, and beautiful figure moved with the ease of an active woodland creature.

" Dora! " cried Archie, leaping from his chair—" hurrah! "

They were but two words, but they administered two separate stabs to Lady Jane Lock. He went forward with both hands outstretched. " How awfully nice of you! " he cried. " Of course you have come to stay —and where's your husband? "

" He's in London," she answered, as Archie

took her long cloak from her shoulders;
"he's tremendously hard at work; and
besides, you know, nowadays one doesn't pay
country-house visits with one's husband."
She laughed at this pertness, but stopped
rather abruptly, aware by this time of the
contrast between her host's effusive welcome
and the general coolness. Leonard Vale
had risen when Archie rose, but had stepped
back instead of forward, and was gazing
at her with his large black eyes from the
obscurity which lay around the lighted tea-
table. She felt that he was looking at her
with a world of meaning, and with a sudden
impatience she turned from him to Mrs.
Dormer, who had not moved.

"Won't you have some tea?" asked Mrs.
Dormer.

"I am afraid I've done a dreadful thing,"
said Mrs. Rutherford, "coming unannounced
like a ghost."

"Oh no," said Mrs. Dormer blandly. "Do
you take cream and sugar?"

"I was so bored in London, and I thought
—but you can pack me off to-morrow, if I
am in the way."

"Nonsense!" cried out Archie; "it's the
most delightful thing in the world, and a
thousand times better than if we had known
about it beforehand. Aunt Susan, you'll see
to Dora's room, and her maid and her luggage
and things, and—and—oh yes, you know
Lady Jane Lock, don't you, Dora?"

"Elizabeth," said Lady Jane, who seemed
not to have heard the reference to herself,
"go and lie down before dinner."

"But I am not tired," said her daughter.

"Nonsense!" said Lady Jane sharply; "you
never know when you are tired."

"How d'ye do, Lady Jane?" said Mrs.
Rutherford.

"Oh! How d'ye do? Such a surprise! I
do envy people who have the courage to do
these odd amusing things. Come, Elizabeth."

"I've plenty of courage," said Dora. She
held out her hand with a smile to Miss Lock,

who was obediently following her mother from the room; and the girl put her hand in hers for a moment. In that moment Dora perceived that Elizabeth's hand was larger than her own, and came to a decision also about her air, her figure, and the cut of her habit. She was extremely quick. As she let her hand fall, she came to a further decision on less obvious matters. " Sulky girl ! " she said to herself; " but how handsome—how dangerously handsome ! "

" I think that I am really the last," said Mrs. Chauncey, advancing from the shadows and looking straight at Archie with a set smile.

" Oh yes ; Dora," he said, " you know Mrs. Chauncey ? "

It was now Mrs. Rutherford's turn to freeze a little. " Oh ! How d'ye do ? " she said, extending her slender fingers.

Mrs. Chauncey pressed the slender fingers slightly, and smiled the more sweetly as she was conscious of a tendency to wring them with all her nervous force. She knew then beyond all possibility of doubt that she hated Dora Rutherford; she would like to wring her neck too, or at least her heart.

CHAPTER VII.

THE news of Archie's danger had come to
Dora Rutherford at a happy moment, for she
was looking about eagerly, almost anxiously,
for something to do. She had been spending
the autumn months in the home of her childhood, the quiet comfortable rectory, which
was so near to the home of Archie's mother,
Mrs. Rayner. There she had been living a
most domestic life with her parents and her
husband. Her husband had been quite happy,
working daily and steadily at that great
report which was to enlighten the world, or
at least a part of it ; but she, for her part,
had found a strange want of occupation. She
could not even take up again the little duties
of her girlhood. Quick, clever, and energetic,
she had taken each year, as she grew up at

home, more and more of the little daily duties
of the house, garden, and village, from the
hands of her mother; but when she married,
her mother had been obliged to take them
back again, and this good lady was wise
enough to know that she would gain nothing
by relinquishing them for a few months, but
the trouble of again acquiring the useful
habits, of which she was now mistress. So
Dora had nothing to do but to visit Mrs.
Rayner, and talk of Archie and his wonderful
change of fortune; or to ride with her husband, when he took his afternoon's exercise;
or to drive her mother in the pony carriage.
Her father, her mother, and her husband
more than all, were busy; but she was idle.
She did not like to be idle. She did not like
to feel herself useless. Before the end of the
visit, during which she had seemed to others
a happy presence indeed, bringing sunshine
every day into the shady corners of that
quiet world, she had accumulated so much
spare energy, that she could scarcely help

crying out when she woke in the morning at the thought of the long hours before her, in which she would have nothing to do.

Nevertheless Dora did not allow her parents to suspect that she grew weary of this idle life, nor did she shorten by a single day the long visit which she had promised to them. Unluckily, when the change came, it was no change for the better. When she went up to London with her husband, she found their house and their establishment in excellent condition, and nothing for her to do but to order the daily dinner. Of London in November she had had no experience; and now she did not like it. Her friends were all out of town; and her husband was more busy than he had been in the country. The work which he had undertaken, first for his own enlightenment, and secondly for the instruction of others, was no less than the examination of all the kinds of land-tenure which are to be found on this small earth, and the setting forth of the merits and defects

of each. Luckily there is not very much
earth to be held in any way; and railways
and telegraphs have made our little world so
small, that any little holiday-taker can run
round it and be back before he is missed.
And yet there is enough solid surface to show
various forms of ownership ; and to know all
these forms, and all the effects of each, is no
small work for a man who has a passion for
thoroughness and a deep respect for truth.

Such a man was Tom Rutherford. He
was up to his knees in reports official and
unofficial, in books written in many languages,
in a growing flood of letters from all parts of
the world ; and he set his teeth and worked
through the mass of matter, carefully and
steadily dividing the relevant from the irrele-
vant, and bringing the former to shape and
clearness with a patience and sturdy determination which was all his own. In this work
of her husband, who shut himself up alone
morning after morning, Dora Rutherford had
no share. When she had ordered dinner,

she felt that she had nothing to do for the rest of the day. She was restless and uneasy ; and so it happened that when she received Leonard Vale's letter and learned that Archie, the only friend of her childhood, the innocent unworldly being whom she had taken under her protection throughout the last London season, was in imminent danger of matrimony, she awoke with delight as from a weary dream. Here was something for her to do ; she could be of some use after-all ; she heard the sound of trumpets and her eyes sparkled with desire of battle. She ran to try on her armour, and already she saw with her mind's eye the redoubtable Lady Jane Lock roll helpless in the dust. Her husband noted the new light in her eyes, and he did not refuse to let her go. He said that he could not leave his work at present, but would try to join her later ; and if he was hurt by her clear joy at going, he only showed it by renewing the attack on his work with a fresh pugnacity.

Dora Rutherford, when she came into the breakfast-room on the morning after her startling appearance at Langley Castle, was keen as frosty air. She was rather late, for she had run out of doors, glancing about the immediate neighbourhood of the house with all the feelings of a strategist casting an eager eye over a new country. She came in fresh and smiling, kissed Mrs. Dormer, as if she had never a doubt of her welcome, and seated herself with her face to all the windows. Thus she confronted the enemy, for Lady Jane Lock always sat with her back to the light at breakfast time. Mrs. Chauncey too, whom Dora preferred to regard as a foe, had this same habit, which indeed is not uncommon in ladies who are undergoing the ordeal of a country-house visit.

All the men were present at breakfast except Leonard Vale, who after a day's hunting was apt to be even later than usual. Of his absence Dora was instantly aware, for she had decided that her first object must be to

gain from him a clear statement of the present
state of affairs. Until she could secure a
private conversation with Mr. Vale, she
could do nothing but keep a friendly eye on
her dear Archie and be ready to make a
third if necessary. Even this light task was
denied her, for, when she asked Archie, as
they were breakfasting, what he was going
to do, he raised his eyebrows with a look
both humorous and pathetic and said, " My
agent has come for me."

" Poor little boy ! " she said ; " but you must
go like a good boy and not cry."

" You don't know how I am bullied," he
said; " here's Uncle Villiers with a list of
people whom I must see, and the agent with
a list of other sort of people, besides horses
and farmhouses and pigs——"

" And guests," said Dora ; " don't leave
us out—especially self-invited guests like
me."

" Don't call yourself names," he said ; " you
know that you have a standing invitation

from me, so long as one stone of this ancestral
dungeon stands upon another and Aunt Susan
provides a crust for dinner."

"There, Mrs. Rutherford," said Lady Jane,
"you can't ask for anything more than that."

There was a slight accent on the word
"you;" but Dora answered smiling—

"I didn't ask for that; but I accept it all.
I'll never leave you, Archie."

"And Mr. Rutherford?" asked Lady Jane,
with a snort, which she had intended to be a
laugh.

"He is as fond of Archie as I am," said
Dora; "he will never leave him either. Let
us all swear never to leave him! He has
such big houses and so many of them; it
would be a kindness to him; and we are such
a pleasant party. We will all run after him
wherever he goes. Let us all swear it! You
begin, Lady Jane."

"Thank you," said Lady Jane, rising from
the table; "but *I* never run after people."

"I do," said Dora; "may I run after you

and the agent this morning, Archie? I will promise to be good, and not to speak unless I am spoken to."

" No," answered Archie. " You'd be too distracting. You will see what is left of me at luncheon."

This was useful information for Mrs. Rutherford, and she made a mental note of it, as she finished her coffee. It made her wish the more for the coming of Leonard Vale, for here was a nice open morning, during which Archie would be safe with his agent, and which she could devote to the necessary interview with the ally, who had called her to his aid and who alone could tell her how imminent was the young lord's danger, and what was the present state of the campaign. She was burning to take command.

When she had seen Archie walk away with the agent and had loitered for some time, and had observed that Lady Jane, whose diplomacy lacked delicacy, was keeping a most obvious eye upon her, Dora went upstairs to her room and dressed herself for a walk. Then she went downstairs again very quietly and slipped out of the house, seen by nobody but Mrs. Chauncey, who was of a more delicate order of diplomatists than Lady Jane Lock.

Dora went straight to the kitchen-garden, which she had discovered in her hasty tour before breakfast. She was sure that, when Leonard Vale had once emerged from his own rooms, he would look for her; and she decided that he should find her in the place most fit for confidential talk; and so she chose her ground in the smaller kitchen-garden, where she was enclosed by high walls and could see from any part both of the entrances. Walking up and down beside the most sunny of the walls she became more and more impatient; but she had not long to wait. She saw one of the green doors pushed open; and Mr. Vale came in. She noted his dejected air, before he caught sight of her, and the quick change which came over him when he saw her. He came up the straight path between the borders of old-fashioned flowers with unusual briskness.

"At last," he said, " I've found you."

"I've been waiting for you for the last hour," she said.

" Waiting for me ?" he asked, as if it were impossible that she should wait for such an one as he. There was a nice blending of humility and reverence and tenderness in his tone.

"Of course I was waiting for you," she answered impatiently. "How can I move until I know how things are now? Is there immediate danger ?"

" Immediate danger?" he repeated vaguely.

" To Archie ?" she said.

He had forgotten all about Archie. "Oh yes," he said, " of course—what a fool I am ! I am afraid things are going about as badly as usual."

" Don't talk like that," she said ; "you promised me in London that you would give up talking like a victim of Fate. It is so tiresome."

"I'll try," he said humbly.

"Come on," she said, beginning to walk up the path; "tell me why you think things are going badly for Archie."

He told her of trifling events which he had noticed since Lord Lorrilaire had joined his party, and especially of yesterday's hunting.

"He was with her all day long," he said.

She nodded gravely.

"We must stop that sort of day," she said; "the girl looks well in a habit. Does she look well on a horse?"

"Not bad," he answered; "she is not like you."

This compliment touched Dora Rutherford where her guard was weak; she was proud of her horsemanship; she could not help smiling nor keep her eyes from shining.

"You must keep up your courage," she said: "I see nothing to be afraid of. Archie cannot be thinking of a serious step; he is so natural, so entirely unembarrassed."

"But isn't that his danger?" he asked; "he might be on the very edge and never know it. Another day like yesterday, and Lady J. would be capable of asking him his intentions."

"The next move is mine," said Dora with glad confidence.

Lenny looked at her with admiration. He thought again that there was nobody like her—no woman so brilliant and so charming; his desire to interest her in himself was stronger than ever before.

"I wish I could hope," he said with a sigh; "and I do hope when you tell me to. You remember what you promised me in London? You said you would be my friend."

"Yes," she said; "I promised to be your friend if you would give up bemoaning your fate."

"I have had hard luck," he said sadly;

" you won't mind my saying that. I know it
has been a great deal my own fault ; I have
thrown away my chances. I have tried to
be different since you advised me and
promised to be my friend."

" And I will be your friend," she said ; " I
am here to help you as well as Archie."

" Thank you," he said eagerly—" thank
you." Then he added sadly, " Nobody ever
needed your help so much. This is my last
chance and I owed it to you. It was you who
told Archie of my existence, and that I—
what may I say ?—had not been treated well.
I owe everything to you."

" Oh no," she said, but she liked the sound
of the words. Of all the men who had paid
her compliments during her short experience
of the London Society which had received
her so cordially as the most charming bride
of the day, this man alone had appealed to
her pity, and shown faith in her ability and
helpfulness. The frank compliments to her
looks, which our somewhat uncouth Society

permits, she had put aside half-pleased and
half-embarrassed, and had promptly forgotten;
but the respect for her opinion and the wish
for her advice, which had been constantly
and delicately shown by this handsome ill-
starred youth, had been compliments which
she did not put aside nor forget. There are
men, and not stupid men, whose cleverness is
never roused to anything like its highest
activity but by the wish to please the other
sex. A man of this sort, who in the other
relations of life has shown but small ability,
if he once desire to arouse the interest of a
woman, will exercise an amazing instinct in
his choice of flattery and a tact in its use,
which are denied to women themselves, or to
all but the most rarely gifted. Such a man
was Leonard Vale. He bent his head as he
walked beside her, and assured her with an
air which was almost one of veneration, and
with the sound of truth in his voice, that but
for her he would have been an outcast.

"And if I lose this chance," he said, " I

shall have to go now. It isn't the luxuries and things I care about; I can do without them; I am not quite such a wretched creature that I can't do without that sort of thing. But this is my last chance of saving myself—of being saved by you, if you will save me."

"Don't talk of saving," she said quickly; "you will stay here; I feel sure of it; and you will find better things to do than playing and betting, and running into debt."

"I will try," he said; "but it's a bad world."

"No, no, no," she cried; "it's a good world, and most amusing, and I don't believe that there is half so much harm in it as people say."

"You always say that," he said, smiling sadly; "and it is so right that you should believe that. It would be a vile world that wasn't good to you; you are not like other women."

"Yes, I am," she said; "but we all like to

think we are different, and it is a mercy to think that one can be of some use to somebody."

"You needn't say that," he said; "everybody knows that your husband is one of the fortunate ones, bound to rise, to make a mark in the world, to do everything which a man ought—— "

Here he stopped short, but his eloquent silence pointed the contrast.

"What has that got to do with it?" she asked.

"He can interest you," he said; "lay his plans before you, consult with you, ask your advice."

"And do you suppose," she asked, "that Tom talks to me of his plans and would listen to my advice? He might listen to me if I were a peasant proprietor or a professor of political economy. As it is—— " She stopped short.

"I am awfully sorry," he said after a minute; "I've said the wrong thing; I had no idea that—— "

" That what ? " she asked, standing still and looking at him. He only answered her with his sympathetic eyes. " I am not complaining of my husband," she said shortly.

It was at this moment, when they were standing together in front of the northern wall of the garden, that Mrs. Chauncey pushed open one of the doors for the admission of herself and Lady Jane Lock. Neither Dora Rutherford nor Leonard Vale saw her, and she drew back and shut the door again, when Lady Jane had had time for one good look.

" Let us go back to the house by another way," suggested Clara Chauncey.

" What does it mean ? " asked Lady Jane authoritatively.

" Oh, surely," began Clara, and stopped with a little laugh. " No," she began again, " it really is not ill-natured. Surely you must have noticed it in London : I go out so little myself, but I thought that it was common talk. Surely you know ? "

" I know that he is a most dangerous and scandalous young man," said Lady Jane.

" And penniless," said Mrs. Chauncey.

" What was that shocking story about him ? " asked Lady Jane.

" Oh, you mean the year before last," said Clara ; " poor Mr. Vale ! Nobody remembers a scandal which is more than a year old."

" I know that it was dreadfully disgraceful."

" Oh yes ! " said Clara ; " but he was so young ; they said he didn't know ! "

" Old enough to know better," said Lady Jane, as she stumped sturdily towards the house : " it was cards, or a horse, or something. I never can remember those stupid male scandals."

Lady Jane Lock was a moralist. She disapproved of married women's flirtations, however harmless ; but she could not help thinking that, if Mrs. Rutherford must have an attentive cavalier, it was well that it should not be young Lord Lorrilaire. She had just completed an arrangement of Lord

Lorrilaire's afternoon, which gave her the liveliest satisfaction, and the only thing which she had feared had been the interference of Dora Rutherford.

"It must be time for luncheon," she said, and perceived with satisfaction that she had an appetite.

CHAPTER VIII.

LADY JANE was patiently absorbing a liberal portion of roly-poly pudding, a dish of which she was particularly fond, when Dora Rutherford came in, still equipped with hat and jacket, and very late for luncheon. "So sorry to be late," she said to Mrs. Dormer ; " and who's the pony cart for ? "

" Is there a pony cart ? " asked Mrs. Dormer absently.

" Yes, and there it goes," said Dora, whose quick ears caught the sound of wheels.

Lady Jane looked up from her roly-poly, and Susan Dormer began to laugh a little in her silent comfortable manner. " Jane wanted Elizabeth to see the ruined Abbey," she said, " and poor dear Archie—— "

"Archie! The Abbey! I must see it!" cried Dora.

In a moment she was out of the room, flying down the passage and out of the front door. Down the Avenue she sped like a deer or the lightest of Diana's nymphs. Lady Jane gripped her spoon and fork and breathed hard. How could she go on calmly with that pudding in the presence of such extraordinary conduct? She looked with indignation at her friend Susan, who could only shake her head and laugh.

"Good old Mrs. Rutherford," murmured Tony Fotheringham at the window; "what a constitution she must have!"

Ten minutes later Lord Lorrilaire entered his dining-room laughing, and blushing a little; but he met the inquiring stare of the speechless Lady Jane without other sign of shame. "It's all right," he said; "there hasn't been an accident; it's Dora."

"What's Dora?" asked Lady Jane hotly.

"What isn't Dora?" he said, laughing; "there never was any one like her."

Lady Jane bit her tongue, that she might not say that she devoutly hoped not.

"We pulled up at the first gate," said Archie, "and I jumped out to open it, and I happened to look back, and there was Dora coming like a racer. She does run beautifully."

"Nice feminine accomplishment!" said Lady Jane sharply.

"Yes," said Archie; "isn't it pretty to see a girl run really well?"

"Where's Elizabeth?" asked Lady Jane.

"Oh, they've gone on together."

"Gone on together!"

"Yes," said Archie; "that was what Dora wanted. As soon as she could speak plain, she said that she was dying to see the old Abbey; and so she turned me out and took the reins."

"And you let her?" cried Lady Jane, who found it hard to hide the contempt which she felt for this rich young man.

"She is perfectly safe," said Archie; "I

assure you you needn't be a bit afraid; she drives a great deal better than I do."

"But she hasn't had any luncheon," said Mrs. Dormer.

"She said she didn't want any."

"She'll never find the way," said Sir Villiers.

"I didn't think of that," said Archie; "but at least she is as likely to find it as I was; you know I'm a stranger in these parts."

His invincible good-humour annoyed Lady Jane Lock, who could not perceive in him any signs of disappointment. She had a speech on the tip of her tongue, which she had tried hard to restrain, but now she could hold it no longer.

"It is not as a whip that I distrust Mrs. Rutherford," she said with decision.

Archie turned quickly and looked at her.

"That's all very well as a joke," he said, with a slight laugh; "but of course everybody knows that there's nobody who can be trusted as Dora can. I give you my word you may be perfectly easy about Miss Lock."

"Thank you! I am not at all uneasy about my daughter," said Lady Jane as she walked stiffly out of the room. She was exceedingly annoyed; she had not even had the heart to finish that good pudding. She took herself roundly to task for having lost her temper and offended her host; she, who prided herself on being a good mother, had failed to do her duty as a mother. She went out for one of her solitary walks and came back full of good resolutions. She was able to receive her daughter with a smile, and to thank Mrs. Rutherford in Archie's presence for having taken such good care of her. "I was rather nervous," she admitted with her straightforward air, "till Lord Lorrilaire assured me that you were a safe whip."

"I can drive anything," said Dora cheerfully; "I enjoyed it enormously."

"And the Abbey?" asked Mrs. Chauncey, looking up innocently from her low chair by the tea-table; "is it really such a splendid ruin?"

"The Abbey?" repeated Dora vaguely.

"Yes—the Abbey which you were dying to see."

"Oh yes," said Dora, "the Abbey—we didn't find the Abbey."

"What a disappointment!" said Clara, with her round eyes gravely sympathetic.

"Terrible!" said Dora; "do give me some tea, Mrs. Dormer! It's awfully rude, but I am so hungry; I had no luncheon, you know."

In that afternoon's skirmish the victory had been with Dora Rutherford; and yet she was not wholly happy. She had had a walk and a run and a drive, and she had missed her luncheon; and so it happened that even she was a little tired, and when she had finished her tea, she was glad to go to her room and rest a little before dinner. The curtains had been drawn across the windows, and the room, with its big bed and handsome

old-fashioned furniture, was lighted only, but
most agreeably lighted, by the cheerful wood-
fire on the hearth.   Wrapped in her dressing-
gown and reclining in an arm-chair, Dora
looked lazily into the fire and was glad for
once to rest.   She could venture to repose for
an hour after her first success; she had seen
the girl go to her room before she had
yielded to her own feeling of weariness.
Resting now in that pleasant place and at
that pleasant hour she ought to have been
wholly happy ; but she was not.   She could
not help a feeling of uneasiness about this
girl, whom she was bound to defeat.   During
their drive she had tried to study her, but
she had been baffled by her apparent stolidity.
Elizabeth had shown no sign of disappointment, when her attendant cavalier had been
banished from the pony-cart; and for the
rest of the afternoon she had shown no
emotion of any kind.   To Dora's questions
about indifferent matters she had answered
briefly and with the air of giving the expected

answers to matter-of-course questions. It appeared that she liked London, that she liked the country, that she liked riding, that she should like to go abroad but liked to stay at home, that she liked dogs but did not dislike cats, and that she did not know if she liked parrots or not; she did not hesitate to say where she got her dresses and her jackets. Dora felt no wiser at the end of their drive, and said to herself with conviction that this was a handsome, heavy, stupid girl; but yet a doubt remained. She had an uneasy feeling that Elizabeth might be more deep than stupid, and that she did not understand her. Now Dora Rutherford thought that she could read girls at a glance, and she was impatient under the suspicion that this girl baffled her legitimate curiosity. She would have liked to be perfectly certain that she knew all about Miss Lock and knew that she was in all ways unworthy of her dear Archie; for then she would have fought her campaign with a heart as light as her courage was undoubted.   However, fight she must, and conquer she would.

Her heart was not light, as she sat before that cheerful fire, or at least not so light as usual.   She felt lonely ; she was accustomed to be popular, and she did not like the thought that not a woman in the house was glad of her presence.   She took it as a matter of course that all the men were glad, and especially Archie, the friend of her childhood. And Leonard Vale too was more glad than the others ; she was important to him ; he needed her help ; he respected her opinions. His admiration and respect soothed her as she sat thinking.

And yet she felt lonely.   She missed her husband.   That was a fact, which she recognized with some surprise.   She made a little face at the fire, prompting herself to be aggrieved at her husband's absence, as if he had left her and not she him.   She even said to herself that he might have come too, if he had wished ; and that the land of this

habitable globe would not have run away
while his report thereon was suspended for a
day or two. Yet she could not feel comfortably aggrieved. She could not help thinking
of her husband with tenderness, with melancholy. She put down this uncommon mood
to going without luncheon; but she was not
content with this explanation. She missed
her husband. This was a fact; and, as she
considered this fact again, she began to feel
pleasure in it. She did not care to go beyond
it. She sat curled up in the big chair and
allowed herself to dwell upon the fact that
she missed her husband. It was another
proof, where none was necessary, how deeply
she loved her husband. She had married
him because she loved him. Whenever she
had felt disappointment in her life as a
married woman, she had always gone back to
her love of her husband and to his love of
her. These twin facts are the important facts
of married life; and Dora Rutherford was
wise enough to know this. Looking into the

wood-fire and thinking of Tom, she warmed her heart once again with the assurance that they loved each other; she missed her husband very much indeed and was glad of it, though it made her melancholy.

And yet, when Dora told herself so truly that, where husband and wife love each other and each is sure of the other's love, all disappointments in their life are in comparison as nothing, she began straightway to slip, as she was apt to do, into unprofitable consideration of a certain disappointment. Dora had married for love; but she had not married, as no loving fool, however foolish and however deep in love, has ever married in this world, with an empty head. She had promised to marry Tom Rutherford because she loved him; but it was impossible for this clever, well-taught, and energetic girl to have but one thought. As a fact, she had had many thoughts, when she promised to marry Tom. She had known well that she was marrying a man of uncommon ability, a

strong man whom his elders, if wise, respected, and whom the best of the younger
men looked to as a likely leader.   He was
some fifteen years older than she, and had
given proofs of his ability, which all might
read.   She knew that he had given his
time to study of the state of the world, and
of the theory and practice of politics; that he
had made his studies in no amateur's mood,
but with steady industry and dogged perseverance; that he had shown great powers of
accumulating and using knowledge.   He had
travelled round the world, too, and had used
his eyes for looking on life as well as on
books.   The occasional papers, which he had
published, had shown mastery of the subjects
on which he wrote, clearness of thought and
of expression; and they had never failed to
attract attention.   He had spoken now and
then on the political questions of the day;
and he had lectured in towns in the North
and had firmly held the attention of North-
country miners and artisans.   He had made

no haste to go into Parliament; but it was generally understood that he could go in at his own time.   Party leaders were well aware of his existence, and even careful to show him no discourtesy.   In any crisis of more than common interest many sensible people looked for the expression of his opinion.   It was known that at the next general election many constituencies would be candidates for his favour, and that some at least would be willing to pay his election expenses.   In short Tom Rutherford, when he was thirty-five years old, was a rising man, and more-over conspicuous among rising men on account of an unusual accuracy of information and the possession of certain settled opinions, which were the result of much study and thought, and which would not be changed, as those who knew him knew well, for the sake of any office or the gain of any votes.   He was not only a rising man; he was a strong man too.

Looking into the fire, and thinking of her

husband and of the place which he was
winning in the world, Dora felt the usual
pride; but it was accompanied, as usual, by
regret. Alone in her room, she blushed and
bit her lip for shame when she remembered
her girlish confidence and her girlish dreams.
She remembered her love and admiration for
her husband, her certainty of his future
greatness, and her certainty that she, the girl
who felt old because she was out of her teens,
would be his chief helper. Once more she
thought how absurd that girl had been with
her belief in herself; and how like a spoiled
child she must have looked in her husband's
eyes. She admitted to herself that she had
been spoiled at home. Her mother was so
fond of yielding, and her father so full of
admiration of his daughter's cleverness; it
was not her own fault if she had been a
spoiled child. And yet, if they had thought
too well of her, that was no reason why her
husband should hold her too cheap. She
said to herself again that her husband did

undervalue her. She knew that she was clever; and she knew that she was well-taught. To doubt this latter fact was to doubt her father, who had been her chief teacher. Did not everybody know that her father had been one of the cleverest men of his day at Oxford, a brilliant scholar and a sound historian too? Did not she know that, when for love and marriage he had settled down into a country rectory and a life of little cares, he had found in time one of the greatest pleasures of his quiet life in teaching his only child to use her mind? She thought of her father with a peculiar tenderness, and remembered without a smile how often he had set forth for her benefit the true theory of education. " I would teach you to use your mind," he would say, " as an athlete is taught to use his muscles ; I do not wish to cram you like a pullet." She recalled this and other wise sayings of her parent, and declared to herself again that filial piety forbade her to regard herself as an ignorant

and ill-taught woman.   And yet had she not
over-valued herself and her ability, and over-
valued herself to a ridiculous degree ?   Back
came the blush to her cheeks as she remembered again that, mere child as she was, she
had held herself fit to help her husband in
his life's work.   She blushed as she remembered her folly, that sublime self-confidence
which her husband had not even suspected.
She had made pompous plans, and had
imagined herself a sort of glorified secretary;
and he had never held her higher than a
petted child.   It was unfair; she was rightly
aggrieved.   So she sat vexing herself again
with this, which was the disappointment of
her married life.   Alone in the firelight and
in melancholy mood she felt much pity for
the young girl, who so few years ago had
gone proudly to be married in the familiar
church at home.   She recalled her folly and
her pride, and then the keenness of the disappointment when she had felt it first.   She
was full of self-pity.   The poor young bride

waking to the fact that she was to be only
loved like any other wife, seemed to her
infinitely pathetic.   And now she told herself that she had never advanced beyond this.
Unfailing love and kindness she had found.
She knew that her husband was a quick-
tempered man—she had seen him angry with
other people; but she had never found him
even impatient with her, except when in
their early days she had come into his study
during his hours of work.   Her offers of help
he had treated as a joke, not even to be
refused in words; he had kissed her and
laughed.   She had realized so soon (she was
clever enough for that) what he expected
from her.   She was to have as many pretty
things as he could afford to give her ; and
she was to have plenty of good society,
which he, who was connected with many
potent families, could give her without undue
trouble.   She had found soon that it was no
use to beg him not to bore himself with so
many dinners and dances, for he had made

up his mind that these things were due to her; and, when he had made up his mind, he went through amusements with the same dogged perseverance which he brought to his graver labours. And she had enjoyed herself, having a fine capacity for enjoyment, making friends of men and women, thinking the best of everybody. She did not deny that she had had great fun; but she was at least as sure that she had not got over, and never would get over, her great disappointment. She was sorry for herself and half-angry with her husband; she knew that she was no fool; and it was her husband's fault that she appeared to the world to be no more than a silly young married woman. For silly young married women she had a supreme contempt. Then Dora thought that it was well that everybody did not think her a fool. Her rapid mind was in search for comfort for her wounded vanity. Other people, even men, cared to listen to her opinions, and even to ask her advice. And so her mind came round again to Leonard Vale. She sat musing for a while, and then suddenly jumped up, looked at the clock on the mantel-piece, dashed off a note to her husband merely to say that she missed him, rang for her maid, and dressed with great speed. When she entered the dining-room, she looked even more radiant than usual, with a deeper flush on her cheek and her eyes dancing. All the evening she was in the highest spirits.

CHAPTER IX.

"Do you know," said Dora to Archie on the next morning, "that I quite like your friend Mrs. Chauncey?"

"Eh? What?" said Archie absently. He was standing with one foot on the fender opening the morning's letters, pocketing some with a rueful look, and throwing others into the fire with manifest relief. Dora was standing near. These two were alone in the dining-room before breakfast. It was natural enough that they should be the first to come downstairs in the morning, to begin as it were the life of the day. They both had a happy morning look.

"I was saying," said Dora emphatically, "that I quite like your friend Mrs. Chauncey."

"My friend?" asked Archie, throwing the

last letters into the fire, and pressing them
down with the poker. "I didn't know she
existed till I found her here.   Who is she?"

Dora laughed. "It's too funny of you," she
said, "to know nothing of your own guests.
Have you no curiosity?"

"Lots," he answered; "but somehow I
haven't thought of Mrs. Chauncey.   Who is
she?"

"Wife of Mr. Chauncey," said Dora drily.

"She's not a widow, then?   I took her
for a little quiet sort of widow."

"Quiet!" repeated Dora, with a slight
peculiar emphasis.

"She seems to me to make eyes, rather,"
remarked Archie sagely.   "Doesn't she?"

"No; there you wrong her," said Dora;
"she has the sort of eyes that make themselves
—men can't discriminate in these things.   Of
course she knows that her eyes are effective."

"Well?   What's the matter with her,
anyway?" asked Archie.

"Nothing that I know of," said Dora;

"but of course one can't have been about in London for the last two years, as I have, without hearing stories."

"Oh, never listen to stories," said Archie bluntly.

"That's what I mean," said Dora. "I like her much better than I thought I should. I always do find people, when I come to know them, a great deal better than people say."

"You are quite right there," said Archie cordially. "People never are half so bad as they are said to be. As for Mrs. Chauncey, she is a little mousie kind of woman; there's no harm in her."

Dora pursed her lips; she felt that it was absurd of Archie to think that he knew. "Anyway," she said, "I choose to like her. She came and talked to me last night after dinner, before you men came in; she quite touched me. She didn't complain; but I am quite sure that her husband is a horrid drinking, gambling sort of man."

"Oh, you haven't come to know Chauncey,"

said Archie, smiling; " when you do come to know Chauncey, perhaps you will find him too a great deal better than people say. You always do, you know."

" Never," said Dora ; " I detest Chauncey, and I hope I shall never set eyes on him."

" That's not fair," said Archie.

" I don't care, and I wish you would not argue before breakfast," said Dora.

" Are you hungry ? " asked Archie ; " let's ring and have up breakfast. I suppose I may ? "

She laughed for answer, and he rang the bell.

While she was being discussed in the dining-room, Mrs. Chauncey in the privacy of her own apartment was putting careful finishing touches to her appearance. That clear pallor, which she accepted from Nature, required nevertheless some skilful management; and about the expressive eyes there was delicate work to be done, that they might be the more expressive. She had, too, a

reputation for wearing clothes well, and
this reputation makes necessary many careful
looks and artful touches.   All had not gone
quite well that morning, and Clara's docile
middle-aged maid was pink about the eyes, and
sniffed occasionally, as if oppressed by unshed
tears.   Clara was thinking of Dora.   She
was well aware that she had advanced in her
favour on the previous evening.   She congratulated herself on this gain.   She was able
even to feel a little virtuous for having been
so nice to a woman, whom she cordially
disliked; and yet at bottom she knew well
that she only cared to win Mrs. Rutherford's
confidence that she might have a better chance
of hurting her.   She was surprised by the
liveliness of her own aversion.   Dora's
happiness affronted her.   Her careless glance
seemed to tell her that she was a faded woman,
and unimportant.   She longed to make this
brilliant young creature in all her insolence
of freshness and youth feel that she too was
somebody.   Besides, she had another cause of

dislike, of which Dora was entirely ignorant.
She had met Tom Rutherford some years
before his marriage, and had practised on him
her artless fascinations; and of these fascinations Mr. Rutherford had remained unconscious to this day, as unconscious as his wife.
And now these Rutherfords exasperated her,
and stung her where she was most tender.
The man was a rising man, whose career was
full of interest; and she thought of her
husband drifting about on the Mediterranean,
and in doubtful company. The woman had
been welcomed with delight into that particular circle of society to which Clara in
more sanguine days had determined to belong.
Political and social success seemed to her
jealous eyes to be made flesh in these
Rutherfords. She had formed no plan for
injuring Dora. She was of that modern
school of diplomatists, who achieve their
ends by refusing to look beyond the next step.
For Clara the next step was to win Dora's
confidence; on this she concentrated all her

powers. She refused to consider what the next step would be; she did not even confess to herself that it would be necessarily injurious to Dora; she was able, as has been said, to feel that it did her some credit to be agreeable to a woman, whom she disliked so bitterly. And yet she knew in her heart that her purpose was to do Dora Rutherford as bad a turn as might be.

In the comedy, which was being played in the house, Mrs. Chauncey was determined to take no part; for consideration had only strengthened her first impression, and she saw clearly that it would be folly in her to run the risk of being condemned by Mrs. Dormer and Lady Jane Lock, that she might help to save one young man from matrimony and another from losing his good quarters. Leonard Vale, though he was an old friend, must take care of himself; she would take no part in that contest. But now she had a little game of her own to play; she would go on step by step; her life had become suddenly more interesting. She smiled at herself in the glass, a timid sad sweet smile, and noted its effect; and then with the smile on her lips, she went lightly down the stairs, leaving her maid behind her, now sniffling with greater freedom, and dropping by mischance a large tear on the gown, which had failed to give satisfaction.

Dora Rutherford looked up from her breakfast as each man entered the room, and noticed certain trifles at a glance which would have escaped a duller eye. She decided from their clothes that no form of sport was purposed on that day; and she knew the full importance of this fact. She was well aware that in a country-house party, where no definite occupation is provided, the danger of matrimony is at least doubled. There had been a day's hunting, but it had been an easy sociable day, and the young lady had joined in the chase; and now it seemed as if day after day there was to be nothing to do. If it be true that Hymen

finds some mischief still for idle hearts to do,
here was too fair a field.   If this had been a
shooting party, Dora knew, though she had
seen so little of the world, that competition
would be for something other than the smiles
of women and jealousy caused by something
other than a girl's kindness.   She had seen
men silent and moody, when they were
expected to be attentive, for reasons which
seemed to her to show the unreasonableness
of men; they had not shot up to their form
forsooth, or more pheasants had gone over
somebody else.   But this party was of the
most perilous kind.   Not only was it full of
daily dangers, and each hour given up to
both the sexes; but it seemed also to have no
necessary end.   Dora without direct inquiry
had discovered that no one of the guests
had been asked for a definite period.   Not
one had been asked from a Tuesday to a
Saturday; nor was a word said by any one
of them, which tended to show that he or she
was on a round of visits.   Such a party

seemed to Dora as if, like a novel, it could only end in an engagement. She saw all the danger ; but the keener her perception of the danger, the more gallant arose her spirit. Noting the signs of this perilous idleness in the men, she only felt the joy of battle. " What are you going to do to-day ? " she asked Archie, as if she had no care but to end one of those periods of silence, which are too common at the breakfast-table.

"Nothing," he answered pleasantly, " unless you can suggest something."

" How is it that you are not shooting at all ? " she asked again.

" My keeper won't let me," he said.

She laughed and looked about her.

" He doesn't mean me," said Sir Villiers drily, as her eye met his; " he refers to the gamekeeper."

" A most alarming man," said Archie, " from Yorkshire, of few words, but very emphatic. He has decreed that we are not to shoot this week."

"But why?" asked Dora.

"I didn't dare to ask," answered Archie; "I suppose the pheasants prefer it. They might give us a chance—or me, at least. I never had much shooting, as you know."

"Good old Archie!" said Tony Fothering-ham kindly; and he added thoughtfully, "All that business with the rifle in America will have made you more out of it still."

"It's very hard on Mr. Tony, isn't it?" said Dora to Archie.

"Oh, never mind me," said Tony.

"Oh, but I am sure it is so bad for you," she said; "I am sure you need a great deal of air and exercise."

"Do you think so too?" he asked, with a sudden accession of gravity. He looked earnestly from Mrs. Rutherford to his well-filled plate. "That's what my doctor says," he added.

"Your doctor!" said Dora; "have you got a doctor?" Looking at the smooth rosy face before her, she could not help laughing.

"You bet I have," said Tony gravely. "I go to Moody."

"Dr. Moody is a very clever man," said Mrs. Dormer, who had become deeply interested at the moment when the conversation touched health; "he was my doctor once—no, not my last doctor; he was the last but two; I can't remember why I left him; I know he is extremely clever."

"He is extremely clever," said Sir Villiers Hickory; "he has made a large fortune by telling people not to over-eat themselves; that's clever."

"It's most important," said Mrs. Dormer.

"Well, I am all for shooting," said Dora; "I am sure that Mr. Tony's health requires it."

"Then you must ask the keeper," said Archie, laughing.

"Well," said Mrs. Dormer, who thought it time to put a gentle end to this plan, "I am sure that I for one am glad that there is to be no shooting this week. One either doesn't see a man all day, or else one has to stand outside a damp clump with poor little rabbits bolting under one's petticoats and great pheasants falling on one's hat, and explosions going on ; and one lunches in a draughty place with guns in all the corners, and a horrid man on each side of you with pockets full of cartridges."

The expression of Mrs. Dormer's views ended the discussion. Dora discreetly said no more; and Mrs. Dormer did not think it necessary to add that the keeper's decision about the shooting had been made after her last friendly visit to the keeper's wife. The Yorkshire keeper had married a little woman, who had been born and bred in a southern county; and, if he were inclined to issue orders to the rest of the world, she was able for the most part to provide him with directions. She and Mrs. Dormer were very old friends, and, if they agreed that not a gun should be fired, the interests of neither owner, keeper, nor pheasants were of much weight in comparison.

CHAPTER X.

Soon after breakfast Dora was standing on the terrace, and looking over the fine expanse of park. It was a broad terrace, stretched in front of the long Italian wing, which was the most modern part of the Castle; and from this raised plateau she looked far away over land, which looked as if every clump of trees, almost every tree, had been planted to make the best possible effect, and as if the land itself had been curved and hollowed in strict agreement with some pedant's rules of beauty.

Since there was to be no shooting, Dora had asserted promptly that, when she was in the country, she liked to be out of doors all day long, and had asked Archie to show her the place; and she now waited for him with some impatience. After a few minutes he came; and she saw that a small company was coming with him. There was Leonard Vale, and Tony Fotheringham, and Mrs. Chauncey, and finally Elizabeth Lock. Miss Lock had said that she had letters to write, but her mother had said " Nonsense ! " and had added that a walk was just what she wanted. As they came towards her, Dora again said to herself that this was a sulky girl.

" I wondered if I might come too," said Clara Chauncey, as if she looked to Dora Rutherford for permission.

" Of course you may," said Dora pleasantly ; " that is, you have as much right anywhere as I have—or more, for you didn't invite yourself." Then she took possession of Archie, giving a little shake to his arm. " Now, Archie," she said, " you are to tell us all about it—the house and the park and every-thing."

" All I know," said Archie blandly; he too stood and looked across this well-kept park. " It must be rather jolly in summer,"

he said; "it looks as if it had been all done
with a spade and a foot-rule, and yet I saw a
bit of land high up in the Rocky Mountains
which looked like this, though of course it
was just as Nature placed the grass and trees.
I suppose this has been pretty well groomed,
though."

"And the house?" asked Dora, giving his
arm a little pull that he might be brought to
regard his stately dwelling-place. "I know
this part; this is the newest; but which is
the oldest?"

"How should I know?" asked Archie.

"You are bound to," she answered.

"But I give you my word I don't," he
said; "it all looks to me old enough. That's
the good of this old English climate of ours.
Now I dare say this place was built at a
dozen different times, and of different stone
too; and then comes our rare old climate
and damps and stains, and sets the ivy
growing and sticks on the lichen, and there
you are—it looks as if it had grown!

He regarded his castle with a dawning affection.

"But you ought to know more about it," said Dora, as they began to move.

"I think that I know something about it," said Clara Chauncey modestly, "if I may venture to instruct its owner. I have been reading about it in the county book. The tower is the oldest part."

They had come down from the terrace, and they now stopped again and looked at the tower, which was connected by a short wing with the rest of the building.

"How old?" asked Dora.

"Well," said Clara, "it has been much restored, but they say in the book that some of this tower is so old that nobody knows to what period it belongs; they talk about ancient Romans and people of that kind; and the walls are tremendously thick; and there is a staircase in one of them."

"Oh!" cried Dora, delighted, "a secret staircase!"

"Yes," said Clara; "and in behind that shrubbery must be the door. Isn't it, Mr. Vale?"

They all looked at Leonard Vale, who had not spoken. He had been looking very cross, but at this appeal to him he smiled on all the party. "I'm afraid I don't know much about it," he said.

"But of course—I never thought of it," said Archie—"of course the upper end of the staircase must come out in your rooms. You ought to see Lenny's rooms," he said to the others; "he has such good taste; he has made them charming."

"They are on view at any time," said Leonard, beginning to move away.

"But does the secret staircase really come out in your rooms?" asked Clara Chauncey with her innocent air of curiosity.

"I never looked," he said shortly.

"It is really so interesting in the book," she said to the others; "all sorts of people have escaped down it—fugitive priests and cavaliers, and a lady eloping, and—oh, it's really most interesting."

By this time they had passed the other wing and turned the corner of the house.

" This is the side which I like best," said Archie; " it doesn't look so much as if a hundred gardeners had been at work on it a hundred years."

They stopped again and looked. Luckily for them it was one of the soft days of November. There was a feeling of moisture and fertility in the air, a gentle wind and a cloudy sky. Under the influences of the day the landscape had a look of gentle melancholy, and of promise too; one seemed to feel the secret work of Nature in the ground, and to anticipate the far-off spring. On this side of the Castle there was no terrace nor formal flower-beds. The park began at the wall and sloped downwards, with no great steepness, but showing a more broken surface everywhere, until it ended in a line of willows, which marked the little brook in the bottom. Beyond the brook the land rose with less steepness, but that more gentle slope was covered with all which the improvements of many owners had left of an ancient wood. There were trim coverts in many parts of the property, which were better adapted for sporting purposes; but this old bit of woodland pleased the new lord the best.

They descended into the dell.

"May we go over?" asked Dora, with her foot on the end of a tree-trunk, which lay across the little stream.

"If you ain't afraid," said Archie.

"Afraid of what?" she asked. "Of your awful keeper, or of a log of wood, or what? Don't you know that I am afraid of nothing?"

"Ah, how I envy you!" said Clara Chauncey, with a devout look in the expressive eyes. "I am afraid of everything. To look at that log gives me a vertigo."

"Then look at me!" said Dora, and she ran along the trunk as safely as a squirrel. "I must go up into the wood," she said from beyond the brook; "it smells so good."

"Stick to the path," said Archie; "and I hope you won't be seized as a poacher. There's a better bridge higher up, and we'll join you."

Dora had begun already to mount the path which led up through the wood. It was a rough track, half-choked with dead leaves and squelchy, as Dora described it to herself, underfoot. She had not gone far when she was aware of some one following her, and, turning, saw Leonard Vale. "Oh, you came over too," she said.

This is one of those remarks on which comment is superfluous. Lenny, who had not put on boots fit for the country, had been picking his way behind her in a rather comical fashion; but, when she turned, he came to her more quickly. "I hope you don't mind," he said.

" Mind ?   Why should I ?" she asked.
" Only," she added, " isn't it rather rash for
us both to leave them ? "

" That's all right for a few minutes," he
said ; " Tony and Mrs. Chauncey are there,
and they are all together.   It's only for a
few minutes, and a few minutes are so much
to me."

She looked at him quickly and began to
walk on again.

" I am always so awfully afraid of offending
you," he said.   "If I were to say half of
what I feel about you and your friendship,
you would laugh at me."

" No," said Dora ; " I told you I liked to
make friends.   I have always said that it is
all nonsense to say that men and women
can't be friends."

" And you will be my friend ? " he said.

" Yes, yes," she answered ; " I told you so."

They walked on together for a time in
silence.

" I wonder," he began presently, " if I am

enough of a friend to say something?" He paused as if for permission.

"How can I tell," she asked, "till you say it?"

He smiled, to show his admiration of her readiness. "I can't help thinking," he said, "of something which you said yesterday. I want so much to tell you that I understand and sympathize; and then I think that it is impossible that you should care whether I care or not. I am disheartened when I think of you and of myself."

"What was it I said?"

"It was about your husband, and his not consulting you, and—— "

She stopped him with her laughter.

"I don't wonder that you laugh at me," he said. "It didn't seem a laughing matter to me."

"At least it is not tragical," she said; "it does not do, I can assure you, to look at these things tragically. One can't expect to be understood by one's husband."

He sighed as he walked beside her. " Of course," he said after a time, "you are right, as you always are. It is brave of you to feel that—and wise, too, I suppose. But, after all, it does seem tragic enough to me. You'll laugh at me, of course ; but I can't help thinking of something, which I read some-where, about an Indian throwing away a pearl richer than all his tribe."

Dora laughed, but not quite naturally. " Alas, poor Indian ! " she said lightly ; " after all it was better than hanging it in his nose."

Leonard sighed instead of laughing. " How can one help cursing fate," he said suddenly and almost angrily, " when one sees a man who has got the best thing in the world and doesn't half value it, and when one knows that to another it would be light and life and everything ?—of course you laugh ; I know I am a fool; but I can't help it."

Dora was not at all inclined to laugh. She was uncomfortable, but interested. She had

had no intention of discussing her husband
with another man ; and yet she had slipped
into a half-veiled criticism of her husband.
She felt that she was wrong ; and yet she was
interested. There was a relief in allowing
the grievance of her life, which she had so
long kept close, to emerge a little into the
light, not so far but that she could clap it
under lock and key again in a moment. And
then this young man, this friend, was so
tactful and so careful of her feelings, that she
could venture to discuss with him a matter,
which she would discuss with nobody else ;
and, moreover—and it was this which made
her most bold—she was certain of her power
over him, certain that she could stop him in
a moment, if he said or even looked too
much. Her power over the young man made
her bold, and it pleased her, too, and flattered
her. She suspected that many women had
flattered him ; and he flattered her. Other
women had admired his looks ; she knew that
she did not care at all for his regular features

and languid grace. This spoiled young man came humbly to her for advice and assistance ; and this pleased her very much indeed. But, although she was pleased, she was uncomfortable too. She felt a quality in his adoration which made her uneasy. She realized that it was time to use her power over him, and to stop him now. " Is it far to the top of the wood ? " she asked.

He did not know ; and Dora, who having once begun to ascend a thing could not be happy till she had reached the top, and seen what was beyond, begun to hurry up the path. And so they came to the upper boundary of the wood, and found a country road beyond which was rough open common.

No sooner had Dora seen this than she turned and hurried down again. " We have left them too long," she said.

He smiled as he followed her ; it gave him exquisite pleasure to hear her speak as if he and she were partners in a plot. This pleased him so much, that he almost forgot

to care whether Lord Lorrilaire married or
no, or only cared because the decision of his
cousin's fate would put a stop to this delightful partnership.   He was wise enough to say
no more at this time about himself or about
her.   As they went quickly down through
the wood, he only made a few remarks about
Archie, speaking to her as to a superior
officer, who kindly allowed him an inkling
of her plans.   Her uneasiness vanished; her
spirits rose; she hurried downward over the
fallen leaves to rescue that other young man,
who might be running into danger.

It seemed as if this sage protector of young
men was not a moment too soon.   When
Dora and Leonard Vale had disappeared in
the wood, the rest of the party had walked
along the bank of the little stream.   When
they had reached the little rustic bridge,
Mrs. Chauncey had declared that it looked
no safer than the log below, and had invited
Tony Fotheringham to walk further up the
stream with her.   So Archie and Elizabeth

had crossed with no other companions and had walked slowly back to where the little track ran up into the wood. There they had waited for Dora's return ; and presently, since she did not come, Elizabeth had suggested that they should return to the house. She would not go back to the bridge again ; she chose to walk the tree-trunk, as Mrs. Rutherford had done. So she had stepped boldly on to the log and walked half-way across, and there had been seized with a sudden panic, had stood still, shut her eyes, and, before Archie had seen that anything was the matter, she had slipped from the uncertain bridge and splashed in the stream.

When Dora emerged, keen-eyed and anxious, from the wood, the sight which she saw was this. On the top of the opposite bank was Archie, wet almost to the shoulders. He had just scrambled up, and was now helping Miss Lock to climb out of the water. The girl's hat was floating down the brook, and a great strand of her splendid hair was hanging loose. When Archie had brought her safe to the top of the bank she covered her face with both her hands and seemed to sway, and would have fallen, perhaps, had not Archie held her in his arms. This was the sight which Dora saw; this was the sight which lent her wings. She darted along the log, and, as she gained the farther side, uttered a shrill cry and fell.

At the sound of Dora's cry Elizabeth awoke to her position; with one hand she pushed back her fallen hair, and with the other pushed her supporter almost angrily away. Archie, seeing in a moment that Elizabeth could stand alone, left her and ran to Dora. Almost at the same moment Leonard Vale, who had stood speechless and sick with fear, appeared at her other side; he seemed to have lost control of himself; he sank down beside her babbling and trembling. "Oh, oh!" he gasped, "she'll die—she'll die, I tell you!" he was ghastly white and his fine teeth were chattering. Archie looked quickly at him with surprise, annoyance, a new dislike. He stooped and lifted Dora from the ground, and by the same movement drew her away from the youth who was grovelling at her side.

As she felt herself raised from the earth Dora opened her eyes and saw that it was Archie, as she hoped, who had raised her. "Thank you," she said feebly, but holding his arm most tightly; "it's better now."

"What's better?" he asked.

"My ankle. You must help me to the house. Oh, thank you, Archie; how good you are!"

She turned her face from his to smile upon Elizabeth, who now drew near to offer aid. "I will take an arm of each of you," she said; and, so supported, she limped up to the house.

CHAPTER XI.

On the next morning there was sound of determined knocking at a door in the tower wing. Tony Fotheringham was there, grave and business-like, arrayed for the chase. He listened, but could hear no sound; and so, after a fit interval, he opened the door and went in.

The room, which he entered, was the middle one of the three, which Leonard Vale had rescued from disused targets, broken bird-cages, and all the strange worthless lumber which a great house must push into some corner. This had been no incomplete conversion. Chairs of divers shapes, each an experiment in comfort, filled much of the floor, and small tables were so placed among them that the most lazy of loungers need move nothing but an arm, and that not far, to the desired tumbler or box of cigarettes. It was, in short, the most luxurious of smoking-rooms; but on the mantelpiece, instead of pipes or tobacco-jars, were bits of fine china, and here and there against the wall stood a piece of valuable old furniture. Opposite to the door was a large window; and in the thickness of the wall a deep window-seat had been made, that the amateur might recline at ease and please his eye with easy seeing of one of the finest views which Langley Castle could give. Leonard Vale had a pretty taste. The smaller room on the right of this was more distinctly a cabinet of curiosities; and in his bedroom on the left, which was under the empty open apartment at the top of the tower, such commonplace things as a young man's washing-stand and chest of drawers were each a bit of cabinet-work which challenged the attention of the earnest inquirer, and made simple folk wonder where the basin could be.

Tony was in no mood to linger over works of art. He walked across the sitting-room and knocked again upon the door of the bedroom. This time a sound of some sort was heard, and, after waiting for a minute to consider its meaning, Tony opened the door and entered. A silken *portière* opened with the door, and, by the light thus admitted from the outer room, the visitor was able to see the bed, at the foot of which hung a piece of needle-work, worked in a harem, sold in the bazaar of Smyrna, and now protecting by day the couch of Mr. Leonard Vale.

Leonard was awake. Without moving his head on the pillow he turned a lack-lustre but hostile eye on the intruder; he said nothing.

"Oh! old chap, I say!" said good Mr. Fotheringham, for the sight grieved him. "It is so awfully bad for you, you know," he added sadly. As Mr. Vale made no comment on this speech, Tony spoke again. "I said I'd come and look you up," he said. "You ought to have breakfasted, you know; the trap is just coming round, and Archie told me to remind you that a horse had gone on for you."

"I wish you had gone on!" said Leonard malevolently. "Ring, will you?"

"What for?" asked Tony, suspiciously.

Leonard growled. His friend regarded him sadly. He sighed and shook his round head before he spoke again.

"I say, Lenny, old chap, I do wish you wouldn't go on like this. You go too fast, you know; you can't last."

"Who wants to last?" cried out Lenny, with sudden liveliness and a more audible malediction. "Do you think I want to save myself up like a pound in an old woman's stocking? *Will* you ring that bell?"

"You drink too much and you smoke too much. My doctor——"

"Hang your doctor!"

"Oh no, I say, don't say that. He is a tremendously clever chap, and he knows."

" Oh, go to—— "

" No, I shan't. I shall tell you what my doctor says. He says you ought not to smoke more than two cigars a day, or their equivalent in cigarettes." The word "equivalent" was invested with an extraordinary solemnity by Mr. Fotheringham. He paused that his friend might have time to digest this golden rule, and then said, " You know, old man, there's nothing more important than health. Do you know my exercise?"

As no answer was returned, Tony gravely inclined his body forward from the hips, and with his shoulders forced backwards to an unnatural extent, uttered in a deep tone the words " Ninety-nine !"

Leonard Vale looked at him with amazement and anger.

"Ninety-nine, ninety-nine, ninety-nine," said Tony Fotheringham, absorbed by this enchanting occupation.

" Great Scot !" said Leonard, when at last the other paused, and looked at him with beaming face, expecting sympathy. "By George, you are a fool!"

"Good old Lenny!" said Tony amiably in answer. "But really and truly, if you will do that exercise for an hour a day, you will be a different man. And as to drink, my doctor says—— "

"Confound you! Will you ring that bell?" cried Leonard.

Mr. Fotheringham rang the bell with a protesting air; and with the same air he heard Mr. Vale's man ordered to prepare the usual pick-me-up. When Leonard had swallowed this dram, he felt more equal to the duties of the day, and listened, while Tony told him again that they were just going to start, and that among the horses, which had been sent on, was one for him.

"Am I fit to go hunting?" asked Leonard plaintively. He put his arm out of bed and held it up and watched it tremble.

"It would do you good, old chap," cried Tony heartily.

" It's a funking day with me," said Leonard;
" my nerves are all over the place; I couldn't
sit on for shaking."

" Well, are you coming ? " asked Tony;
" we can't wait. Archie told me to remind
you, if you weren't ready, that you could
order the dog-cart, and come after us and
take your chance."

" Who's going ? " asked Leonard.

" Well, there's me, and Archie, and good
old Hickory and Mrs. Rutherford."

Leonard Vale threw off the clothes and
brought his feet to the floor. " Oh, I am
bad," he said miserably, as he sat on the bed
—" I can't go; it's no good; it's just my vile
luck." He turned into bed again, stretched
down a long left arm to pull up the bed-
clothes, and lay with his face to the wall.

Tony waited a moment, regarding his
prostrate friend with a pathetic expression
on his rosy face.

" Oh, do get out, can't you ? " growled the
friend; and Tony went.

Tony, descending sadly from the tower wing, found the rest of the party assembled near the fire in the hall. Had he been quick at perceiving the moods of others, he would have seen that Lady Jane Lock was but little happier than the friend, whom he had left cursing destiny upon his bed. The lady was very stiff in the back and very red in the face, and, do what she could, she could not restrain her tongue entirely from speech. The sight of Mrs. Rutherford descending the majestic staircase, wearing a perfect habit, and moreover displaying on each step the neatest of riding-boots, had filled Lady Jane with a wrath, for which some vent was merely necessary. A sprained ankle on one day, and such a boot on the next! She had tried hard not to speak, but at last she was forced to say something. This something took the form of congratulation. " I cannot help congratulating you," she said, with a sort of strangled laugh, " on your wonderful recovery, or rather on your wonderful ankle."

Dora smiled sweetly upon her, and looked down at her foot with an exasperating approval.

"I should think there never was such a case," continued Lady Jane, who was hurried away by her own words; "a miraculous cure of a sprain—it really ought to go to the medical journals."

"To tell you the truth," said Dora, with enchanting candour, "it was really nothing at all."

"Really?" asked Lady Jane, with concentrated scorn.

"I was more frightened than hurt," said Dora; "and I am so glad it was no worse, for I wouldn't have missed to-day for anything. I do hope that Miss Lock will be all right when we get back."

It was beyond the power of Miss Lock's mother to express gratitude for this kind wish. While Dora, radiant and in closely-fitting boots, was about to start with the men for a day's hunting, poor Elizabeth was in

her room, suffering from a chill. Her mother
had stood beside her bed, regarding her with
the eye of an army doctor who suspects a
recruit of shamming. She had rated her for
her clumsiness, as if she had fallen from a
bridge edged by high parapets for the safety
of passers. She had administered a dose,
which she had brought many times to the
bedside of every one of her daughters; and
finally she had stoutly declared that the best
remedy for this chill, which ought never to
have been taken, was a day's exercise in the
open air. Not a word had Lady Jane Lock
said of her objection to girls' hunting; she
was ready to pocket her prejudices for the
good of her child; she was eager to hoist her
into the saddle. But Elizabeth would not.
She would not hunt—she would not even get
up. Is it to be wondered at that Lady Jane
was unable to refrain from bitter speech,
when she saw Mrs. Rutherford radiant, attrac-
tive, admirably equipped for the chase, and
thought of her own child, who positively

rejected her advice ? " Elizabeth is obstinate as a mule," she had said, not for the first time, to her friend Susan Dormer. " Elizabeth has so much character," she was apt to say confidentially to less intimate acquaintance. Express it as she would, she was well aware that this girl was able to meet her will with a passive opposition which she had not found in any of her elder daughters. She had not encountered this opposition often ; but, when she had encountered it, she had found, as she found on this day, that Elizabeth had her way. This element, so little expected in a daughter of hers, embarrassed Lady Jane more than all the other obstacles which barred her path. She was like a skilful chess-player, who has suddenly found to his amazement that the most important of his pieces may refuse to move. Imagine the attitude of a player, who awakes to the doubt if his queen have not a will of her own ! To such a doubt Lady Jane had been growing more and more alive since the day on which she had presented at Court the youngest and hand-somest of her daughters.

The day's hunting was better than the last ; and Dora, happy in the country air and glowing with the ardour of the chase, forgot, save at brief moments, all plots and counter-plots, and the important duty of saving the young men, her contemporaries. She enjoyed herself like a child, and could not believe that the sun was not sloping to the west before his time. Archie was not joyous enough to please her ; and she again and again demanded from him more expressions of his happiness. When they were riding homeward together, she attacked him on this subject.

" Why so glum ? " she asked.

He laughed, and denied that he was not jolly.

" You are not half such good company as you used to be," she said.

" Perhaps I'm growing old," said Archie.

As she considered his unusual solemnity,

the full perception of his danger came back to her. She was half inclined to follow up her attack, to put this matter to the touch, to ask him suddenly then and there if he were glum because Elizabeth was not there. The question was on the point of her tongue; but it came no further. She decided that it would be rash; she gave full weight to the fact that, in spite of all their old friendship and old interchange of thoughts, he said not a word to her about this girl. She could not believe that he did not think about her, especially since he had pulled her out of the brook, and seen half her hair down; and yet he did not speak about her. This fact appeared to Dora significant of much; and she made up her mind not to begin discussion of this perilous subject. She was not too much elated by her little victories; for she knew full well that, if the mischief were already done, to carry off the young man day after day, was but to feed the flame. The absence, which makes the heart grow fonder,

is generally a short absence.   So Dora thought
and determined to check her natural impetu-
osity, to be cautious, to say nothing yet
about Elizabeth.

"I was thinking of old Palfrey," said
Archie presently; "I was wondering how
one entertains a man who is going to be in a
Cabinet."

"What? Mr. Palfrey? The great Mr.
Palfrey? Is he coming here?"

"We shall find him when we get back,"
said Archie, nodding.

"But who asked him? What's he coming
for? Do you know him?"

"No, I don't know him," said Archie;
"how should I? He's to speak at Langstone
next week."

"But who asked him to stay with you?"

"Uncle Villiers. Do you object, Dora?
Shall I thrust him from my gates?"

Now, Dora was busily thinking whether
she objected or not. So far as the danger of
matrimony was concerned, the infusion of a

lively political element was a thing to be
welcomed. And yet it vexed her that the
friend of her youth, her dear Archie, the
potent young Lord Lorrilaire, should be
nobody in his own house.

"They say that an Englishman's house is
his castle," she said, with her chin in the air.

"Well?" asked Archie.

"Your castle seems to be everybody else's
house," she said; "that's all."

He laughed in the best humour. "They
take all the trouble," he said.

"And besides," she went on, "you are a
Liberal. Why should you entertain one of
the rising lights of the other people?"

"They are much of a muchness," said young
Lord Lorrilaire; "I'd about as soon feed one
as the other."

"No, no, no," cried out Dora; "that's
nothing in the world but laziness. I thought
you'd say that sort of thing, and it's only
laziness! You ought to take a side. There
must be more right on one side than another.

You can't not care about politics ; and you are a power in the land ; you must take a side and stick to it."

" Is that necessary, nowadays ? " asked Archie, laughing ; " I mean the sticking to it ? "

" Of course you can be flippant," said Dora ; " but of course I am right. A man ought not to let other people make him into just what they like."

She said this with decision, and she paused when she had said it, that he might take from it as much profit as he would.

" There's no fear," said Archie after a time ; but she shook her head.

" One can put one's foot down at any time," he said again ; but again she shook her head.

" Well," he said, laughing, " let us float a little way ! I assure you, Dora, I don't feel yet as if my life was real. Sometimes all this sort of thing seems a dream ; and sometimes all the old time seems a dream ; but I can never believe in both at once. You must give me time to feel my feet. Feeding Mr. Palfrey for a few days can't make me a Tory, if there are any Tories; and——"

"And what?" asked Dora quickly.

If Archie had been on the point of adding a statement even more interesting to the lady, he thought better of it. He laughed instead; he always found it so easy to laugh, and to laugh is often the least compromising end of a sentence.

"Well, there's the Castle," he said presently, as they came within sight of it; "is it all real or a dream—all this imposing existence?"

Dora answered with a little sound of contempt.

"You'll find it real enough," she said, "when you've floated too far to get back."

"One can always get back," he said, laughing again.

CHAPTER XII.

" Feeding Mr. Palfrey for a few days can't make me a Tory," Archie had said ; and then he had said " and "; and then he had stopped, adding nothing but laughter. Dora, when she was alone in her room, resting and thinking before the dressing-bell, wondered much what words had nearly followed that suggestive " and." She completed the sentence for her own satisfaction in this way:— " Feeding Mr. Palfrey for a few days can't make me a Tory, and admiring a girl's back hair, also for a few days only, can't make me a husband."

Was this what Archie had so nearly said ? If so, why had he stopped ? Had chivalry stopped his tongue, or a sudden doubt if he were not really falling in love ? She tried to analyze his laughter, which had come in the place of words. Was it mere careless laughter, or was there in it some element of tenderness? Had he laughed as a young man laughs detecting in himself a hidden weakness of love ?

Dora recumbent after the fatigues of the hunting day tried to determine the state of her gallant young host; but she failed to satisfy herself. Only of one thing did she grow more sure; the introduction of the political question into Langley Castle was a decided good. Politics, as she told herself, are as good an antidote to love as shooting is. If the one makes men silent and moody, the other makes them argumentative and garrulous. Both turn the minds of men upon each other and divert them from the dangerous consideration of the other sex. So a young man turns from a lady's eyes to discuss local government, of which he probably knows much less.

Dora felt sure then that she might welcome

the advent of politics and of the politician. She made up her mind to receive Mr. Palfrey as an ally. For her own sake, too, she felt a pleasant excitement at his coming. She liked to meet eminent people; this had been among her most favoured dreams in her girlhood's days at the rectory. To meet eminent people, to feel the currents of political life, to be in and of the movement—these had been among the visions of the little daughter of the country clergyman. Many of her dreams had come true; but not the dearest dream of all. Other politicians had listened to her with apparent interest, but not her husband. This, as has been said, was the disappointment of her life. And this disappointment gave a peculiar excitement to each new introduction to an eminent man. She was eager to impress each impressive person; she felt like an Indian with yet another scalp in prospect; and her heart fluttered at the hidden thought that, when all men had acknowledged that she was worth hearing, perhaps her husband last of all might awake to the amazing fact that he had not married a fool.

Now, it happened that Mrs. Rutherford had never met Mr. Palfrey, or, if she had met him at some large official party, she had not known it. She would not have known him by sight but for the shop-windows. Mr. Palfrey had attained to that stage in the life of the politician, which is marked by the sudden appearance of his photograph in shop-windows. The actors, whose likenesses adorn the same windows, appear truculent or benevolent, tender or sinister, according to the characters which they represent ; but the statesmen all wear the same expression. Among them the countenance of Mr. Palfrey had lately appeared. Mr. Palfrey was recognized as one of the rising men of his party.

Dora allowed herself more time than she usually gave to her toilet. When this was well advanced, she sent her maid with kind inquiries about the health of Miss Lock ; and

the maid returned with the thanks of the
young lady and the news that she was much
better, but would not leave her room that
evening.   This, too, was satisfactory to Dora.
She had no wish that Elizabeth should be
ill ; but yet a free evening was something
for which to be grateful.   Of course, if the
girl were really ill, Lord Lorrilaire would
feel pity, and, where there is pity, there is
danger.   But still, as Dora put the last
touches to her charming toilet, she felt a
sense of freedom, the anticipation of a pleasant
evening, of a new success.

As she looked at herself in the big glass,
she admitted with her natural frankness that
Elizabeth was according to rule a handsomer
woman than herself; but fascination cannot
be reduced to rules ; she was content with
her appearance.   She was altogether sanguine.   For that night at least all promised
well.   With a fine flood of politics and the
girl away, a real victory might be won, and
the rich young lord swept clear beyond the

reach of danger. So down went Dora in her most becoming gown and most agreeable mood.

If Dora had suspected that there was a deliberate purpose of penning Lord Lorrilaire in the Conservative fold, she was sure of it when she entered the drawing-room. She recognized Mr. Palfrey in a moment. He was standing by the fire with his head a little bent, and the expression which a prominent politician wears when he is courteously pretending to listen to an outsider, and is thinking of something else. She at once drew his attention to herself, but at the same moment she was aware of the presence of another and an even more remarkable man. She saw Lord Hackbut. Archie had said not a word of the coming of Lord Hackbut; and Dora at once doubted if Archie had known of his coming. It was as likely as not that Sir Villiers had not mentioned it; and yet Dora knew that, if Mr. Palfrey were a sign of an intended capture of Archie, the pre-

sence of Lord Hackbut was a sign ten times
as serious. Lord Hackbut always meant
business.

Lord Hackbut was at least ten years older
than the rising Palfrey, and, so far as the
public knew, he had not yet begun to rise.
Nevertheless he was a man of great strength,
both bodily and mental. If the public knew
little of him and had never seen his harsh
old face grinning from the windows of
stationers and fancy repositories, he was well-
known to the few who were proud of knowing the inner mechanism of the Conservative
party. With these initiated persons he enjoyed the reputation of having refused all the
things which public men as a rule impatiently
demand. He was said to have refused the
highest places about the Court, many special
missions, all sorts of ribands; and many years
ago, in the days of his youth, to have declined
those subordinate offices in Governments,
through which the able man rises in due
course to a seat in the Cabinet. The decora-

tive side of public affairs had never tempted
him, nor to be pointed at by the vacillating
finger of the man in the street ; the magic
words, " That's 'im," had never thrilled his
soul.   It was organization which attracted
him.   From the first he had but one great
aim in meddling with politics—to be admitted
freely behind the scenes, to learn how the
puppets are worked, and in due time to work
them.   He had become the most powerful of
party managers.   He had assisted in the
formation of Cabinets ; he had conducted
negotiations between doubtful colleagues.
He knew more than any man in England of
the strength of the party in this place or
that, and how far that strength would be
increased or diminished by any given policy.
Therefore he was consulted with eagerness
both as to measures and men.   Before the
Caucus had appeared in England, or the
American weed in English rivers, Lord
Hackbut had been a sort of Caucus in
trousers, standing on legs rather bowed and

of extraordinary strength, with massive head
a little pushed forward, and keen humorous
eyes.   A nose, which looked as if it had been
broken, and a front tooth which certainly had
been broken, added a certain fierceness to the
appearance of this remarkable man.

Lord Hackbut was well aware of the
services which he had rendered to his party.
He owed them nothing, and he held that
they owed him much ; but he asked no com-
pensation but the free indulgence of a somewhat sardonic humour.   He worked hard for
his party, and loved to mock the party leaders.
It was of course in private life that he thus
played the mocker.   On the rare occasions,
when in his own county he felt bound to
speak in public, he would so load his leaders
with eulogy so extravagant, that his audience
cheered him and them to the echo, while the
eminent person, who happened to be present
as the representative of the body eulogized,
would wear the constrained and rather painful
smile of one who suspects irony.   Irony is

understood by very few Englishmen, and liked by fewer.

So soon as Dora, entering the drawing-room, saw the marked countenance of the great party manager, she knew that a serious effort was about to be made to brand a doubtful sheep with the right party mark. It was a work after Lord Hackbut's heart to preserve for his party the influence and wealth of a family which had always been given to that party. Dora was sure that he had learned all about Archie, and that he would lose no time in fixing him, where he should be, at the head of the Conservative party in the county. She felt indignation for Archie; but yet she saw, or thought that she saw, more clearly than ever that a definite plot against the young lord's political preferences made the other plot, which was directed against his heart, more likely to fail.

It was clear that the formidable Lord Hackbut was in the highest spirits. The broken tooth was visible each moment. He

took much delight in the society of pretty
women: and he had been surprised and
pleased at meeting his friend Mrs. Chauncey
in that place. She for her part faced him
bravely but warily; she was a little afraid of
the old lord, and of his piercing eyes and
voice. "And where is my friend Jack
Chauncey?" he asked in his clearest tones—
"yachting, is he? Yachting! I thought
that punting was more in his line." He
laughed stridently at his own jest; and Clara
laughed too, though with effort. She was
glad of the entrance of Dora, even though
she knew with her fatal perception that Lord
Hackbut recognized at a glance the appearance of a beauty fresher and more novel than
her own. It was always the next thing that
this alarming peer might say, which made
people nervous in his society.

Lord Hackbut regarded Mrs. Rutherford
with obvious admiration. He took Mrs.
Dormer in to dinner, but he found Dora on
his right hand, and he frankly expressed his

pleasure at the arrangement. It was to Dora that he addressed the greater part of his talk, and he was in a very talkative humour. He informed her at the outset that to talk to a pretty woman was always pleasant; but that to talk to a pretty woman, who occasionally understood what one meant, was one of the rarest pleasures of life. He was outspoken as usual, and amused Dora immensely with his rash speeches.

"I am here," he said, in an interval of his very hearty dinner, "as a hanger-on of the eminent man on the other side of the table. Do you know him? No? You won't hear much from him now. He has a tremendous speech on his chest, which he has got to get off next week at Langstone. Besides, he won't talk before me; he knows that I know what a humbug he is. Look at him now! He knows we are talking about him."

"It is you who are talking about him," said Dora.

"So it is," said Lord Hackbut. "I love to

talk about him. Look at him! Now he is
trying to look impressive, like an engraving
of Pitt; now he is curtseying and condescend-
ing, and pretending to listen. I can tell you
that he looks quite different when he's listening to a Whip or to one of his local Three
Hundred. He's one of the biggest humbugs
in Europe. He tossed up at Oxford to see if
he should be Liberal or Tory. It came down
tails (the heads belong to the other party),
and we got him, and much good may he do
us. Shall you go and hear him speak ? "

" Of course," said Dora; " especially now
when I know all about him."

" Yes, my dear," said the old lord, " you
come to me when you want to know about
these fellows. It's all a fraud, and we are all
in it. Do you believe in popular votes and
all that ? "

" Yes," said Dora; " I'm a Liberal."

Lord Hackbut laughed aloud; and Palfrey
looked across the table with a startled eye
and an uneasy smile.

" He believes in all that," said Lord
Hackbut, nodding at Mr. Palfrey, " or pretends that he does. It's the biggest humbug
in Europe. We wouldn't give any fellows
votes if we could help it. Do you mean to
tell me that I shouldn't govern my county a
blanked sight better than the hat-in-hand
nominees of a lot of agricultural labourers?
Better have given votes to foxes any day—far
more intelligent. Palfrey pretends to believe
in the people ; if he's anything, he's the
biggest Radical in Europe. I bet you he says
' democracy ' in the next ten minutes; and
I'll lay you ten to one he says it in the last
ten minutes of his speech at Langstone—in
public speeches it comes in the peroration."

" Oh, Lord Hackbut," said Dora, " I do
hope you'll make a speech ! That's what I
should like to hear !"

" Only a word or two," he said, "just to
tell 'em what an honour and privilege they
enjoy in listening to the words of wisdom of
the persuasive Palfrey."

Dora was very much amused by her neighbour. Before dinner was over, he asked her a few sudden questions about their young host, which she answered so diplomatically, that he burst out laughing again and declared with emphasis that she was an uncommonly clever little lady. When she rose with the rest of the ladies, he made her a low bow and expressed a hope that they might be friends.

"Yes," said Dora, with a quick look, "and allies too, perhaps, if we can come to terms."

"I ask nothing better," said the old lord gallantly, and displaying his broken tooth.

One thing, and one thing only, interfered with Dora's pleasure on that evening. She was disagreeably conscious of the eyes of Mr. Leonard Vale. She had not seen Leonard on that day until she came down to dinner; and then he had been unable to speak to her. At dinner he had sat far down on the opposite side of the table; but she had felt that he was continually looking at her, and with

variations of expression which annoyed her.
Entreaty, expostulation, and even rebuke
seemed to her to be directed at her from
those expressive eyes. She was annoyed ;
she condemned him for silliness ; she feared
that the keen-eyed old man beside her would
notice those persistent looks. She made up
her mind to speak very plainly to Mr. Vale
when the next opportunity of speaking should
come. Yet, when she had left the dining-
room, she at once rebuked herself for making
mountains out of molehills. She reminded
herself that the young man had confessed
himself a very weak creature, and that she
had promised to befriend him. It was certain
that his looks meant no more than a longing
for another tonic dose of good advice. If she
must find fault with him for staring, she
determined not to speak as if she suspected
an excess of devotion. She declared to herself that that would be foolish indeed, and
would be in short like the behaviour of one
of the silly women, who thought all men in

love with them, and whom she had always
and unequivocally condemned.

And yet, when the men joined them, Dora
was vexed again by the airs of this young
man.   He looked pale, and dark under the
eyes, aggressively interesting.   He made no
determined effort to come to her; but he
continued to stare, till Dora felt as if all the
world must notice his staring.   She gave
him not a glance in return, and tried not to
think of him.   She had almost succeeded in
this effort, and the evening was drawing to a
close, when she rose with some of the others
to go into the next room, that they might
look at a picture there.   As they passed
through the archway from one room to the
other, Dora felt a hand touch hers and a
scrap of paper left in her fingers.   She started
and looked a quick and angry question, but
she only saw the back of Mr. Vale, as he
moved away.   Clara Chauncey, who was
close beside her, began to ask questions with
great interest about the picture; and the

others stopped before it, while Dora moved on alone to the mantelpiece at the end of the room. There she looked at the piece of paper with marked disfavour, and almost instantly allowed it to drop from her fingers on to the coals. When she said good night to the gentlemen, she was careful to make no reply of any kind to the mute appeal of Leonard's eyes. He ground his heel into the carpet and swore under his breath, as he saw her vanish up the staircase.

A little later another female figure, equally light, flitted down the staircase. The gentlemen had disappeared, and the footmen were removing the lights from the drawing-room. Mrs. Chauncey came in quickly and went straight to the fireplace in the further room. " One moment," she said to the man who was moving the nearest lamp; " I won't keep you a moment, but I am afraid I threw a paper into the fireplace by mistake."

The footman held the lamp conveniently near. "I am so sorry to trouble you," said

Clara, who was always polite to other people's servants, " but I foolishly threw a little paper into the fire. Ah, there it is! Yes, that's it; thank you! A little burnt? Yes, so it is; but not much. So lucky that it stuck on the black coals! Thank you!"

Half of the little paper was burnt away; but enough remained. Clara folded it carefully and held it hidden in her little hand as she sped upstairs for the second time. Safe in her room, she locked up the little note in a safe place, and then prepared herself for that repose which chloral, even more surely than innocence, can afford to the nervous female temperament.

CHAPTER XIII.

TONY FOTHERINGHAM slept in a room on the
ground floor; and as a rule he slept like a
good little boy, breathing steadily from the
moment when his round cheek touched the
pillow to the moment when he was called to
resume the diet of the day.   But on the night
which followed the arrival of Mr. Palfrey
and Lord Hackbut, Mr. Fotheringham was
somewhat disturbed.   He turned over more
than once; he even dreamed; half-awake he
thought uneasily of his precious health.
Something, he feared, had disagreed with
him.   He wondered, as he moved his hot
cheek on the pillow, if he had been upset by
the somewhat lurid talk in the smoking-room,
where "good old" Hackbut had denounced
the age with savage speech and much robust

enjoyment. Tony had listened open-mouthed to the awful pleasantries of the old and critical peer; and now he lay wondering if he had gone to bed with his head too hot. It was either Lord Hackbut's picture of his times, or the chestnuts of which he had imprudently partaken after dinner, which was the cause of the rosy boy's disquiet. The light was long in coming. At last he awoke again from uneasy slumber, and there was the morning rosy too.

It was Sunday. Tony left his bed, drew his curtains open, and pulled up his blind; and looking at his watch, he found that there was still more than an hour to be passed before his usual time of waking. It was now clear to him that something was wrong with him. He examined his fresh young face in the glass with solemn interest, and he imagined that he saw therein signs of the commencement of various maladies. Something must be done. He looked out of window again, and felt the temptation of the

morning.   Air and exercise were the cheapest
and easiest remedies within reach.   He would
out into the air, and return to his bath when
the man had put it ready.   Quickly dressing
himself in white flannel, with a cashmere
scarf across his throat, and over all a warm
pea-jacket with its collar turned up to his ears,
he opened his window and jumped down on
to the terrace.   From the terrace he descended
into the park.   A light hoar-frost was on the
grass; the sky was clear but cold; the freshness of the air set the boy's tennis shoes in
motion. Mr. Tony began to trot steadily (he
was there for his health) across the grass in
the direction of the main avenue.

Tony paused when he reached the road
and considered his condition. He found
with pleasure that he was better already; he
congratulated himself on the means which he
had taken to baffle the insidious enemy; he
thought no more of the treacherous maladies
which had seemed close upon him. He
walked briskly along the road and away from

the house, until presently he remembered
how wise it is to vary the form of exercise,
and on the instant his mind jumped to his
own favourite little exercise.   He glanced
this way and that ; nobody was in sight.   So
early in the Sunday morning rest was everywhere ; it was wonderfully still ; not even a
twig was stirring.   Tony moved on to the
rough grass by the side of one of the great
trees which formed the avenue, and under its
protecting arms commenced his strange and
imposing performance.   With his feet firmly
planted a little apart, his body bent slightly
forward from the hips, and his shoulders
braced tightly backward, he began to bend
his knees and straighten them with a regular
rhythmical movement, while as an accom-
paniment to the exercise he uttered again and
again in his deepest tones the suggestive
words " ninety-nine."

Tony was alone with Mother Nature, but
not for long.   Scarcely had he begun to
repeat " ninety-nine " with an unvarying

regularity, when another person appeared upon the road advancing rapidly towards the house. This was a slight young man, but little older than Tony himself, in a great hurry, walking quickly though with short steps. The skirts of his black frock-coat, which was open, floated and fluttered behind him as he came; and his breast-pocket was so full of papers, that it hung heavily away from him, and seemed to draw him from the straight line as he hurried forward. His appearance was out of sympathy with the freshness of the morning and the clean air of the country. London was in his looks; and he seemed to have been up all night. His high hat, which was distinctly too large, had not been brushed since yesterday, nor had his clothes, which were otherwise so respectable. A thick little mat of black hair appeared on his forehead below his hat, and beneath the mat and from the keen pale nervous face a pair of black eyes looked, eager, restless, and feverishly given to observation. It seemed to be of importance to the universe that not a blade of grass should escape those eyes. About the whole man there was an air of earnest purpose and of self-confidence. Indeed, Mr. Beck was always hurrying to put something right; and so many other things were in need of his correcting influence, that it is no wonder that he did not find time to brush his hat.

To Mr. Beck hurrying up the road there was no sign of any less important presence, until, suddenly passing one of the large trees, he came close upon a boyish-looking individual conscientiously exercising himself on the grass. Mr. Beck stopped short with a nervous start, but with no sound; he had taught his nerves not to betray their sudden shock by noise; as an observer, he had found this education of his excitable nerves strictly necessary. He now stood still staring, and the interest which he had encouraged himself to find in all exhibitions of humanity grew strong within him. Here was something the like of which he had never yet seen. His fingers went of themselves to the bulging coat-pocket in which his note-book was buried ; but, when he had dragged it out, he only twisted it about unopened in those same lean, and at present dirty, fingers, while he continued to look and look. He was indeed an observer of life.

Tony had not heard a sound. Any noise which the light tripping feet of the other had made on the road had been lost for Tony in the unceasing repetition of his great formula. " Ninety-nine, ninety-nine, ninety-nine ! " he said, deepening his innocent tones as became the importance of the ceremony, and solemnly rising and sinking with the rhythmical bending and straightening of the knees. It was a rule of Radley Beck never to interrupt the progress of a phenomenon which might lead to more interesting developments. He stood watching with the liveliest interest, till Mr. Fotheringham, at length conscious of this strenuous and compelling observation, stopped between a "ninety" and a "nine," straightened his knees for the last time, and turned and stared in turn.

"Hah!" cried Mr. Beck in a high voice.

"Eh?" said Tony, rather shamefaced.

"May I ask the meaning?" asked Radley Beck, speaking quickly and with a certain precise pronunciation of words, which he had brought from Oxford and had not yet lost in London. "Is it a local form of religion? Survival of some country superstition? Sunday morning—by the roadside—sun-worship still to the fore—Ninety-nine what?" He seemed to be murmuring the headings of some paper. "Ninety-nine what?" he asked of Tony, smiling friendly and inquiring.

"Oh, it's only a little sort of an exercise," said Tony, abashed by the extreme interest displayed in those eyes; then, as enthusiasm rose again within him, he added, "It's wonderfully good for you, you know—for the lungs and that."

"It is extremely interesting," said Mr.

Beck, with his head on one side; " doubtless you are a guest at Langley Castle ? "

" Yes," said Tony.

" Is Lord Lorrilaire there ? "

"Oh yes, he's there right enough," said Tony.

" Names of other guests ? " said the stranger, inclining his head again towards his left shoulder.

" What ? " asked Tony.

" Will you favour me with the names of the other guests at the Castle ? So glad I met you."

" Thanks," said Tony ; " but what do you want their names for ? Are you a reporter ? "

Mr. Beck smiled a smile full of meaning.

" Yes and no," he answered, " as we used to say at Balliol. I am a friend of Lord Lorrilaire."

Tony Fotheringham looked at the other with surprise, which was hardly complimentary.

" Well," he said, with some hesitation, " it

you are a friend of Archie, of course—well, there's Mrs. Dormer for one, and there's good old Hickory for another—Sir Villiers Hickory, you know—and Mrs. Chauncey, and me, and Lenny—— "

Mr. Beck, who had received each name with a little nod, here interrupted to ask who Lenny was; and hearing that it was Leonard Vale, he asked again with keener interest if it was the Leonard Vale about whom there had been a story.

"It was hushed up," he said; "yes; kept with some difficulty from the press."

"Oh, that was last year," said Tony.

"Quite true," said Mr. Beck; "no further public interest." After a moment he added, "And Lady Jane Lock is of the party with a daughter ?"

"Yes," said Tony.

"Is a marriage probable ?"

"Can't say," said Tony.

Mr. Beck wagged his head at him with a knowing manner.

" Is that all the party ? " he asked, peering keenly at Mr. Fotheringham.

" That was all," said Tony ; " but now there's old Hackbut and Mr. Palfrey."

" Hah ! " cried out Mr. Beck with his highest note.

" What's the matter ? " asked Tony rather crossly.

" And Lord Lorrilaire ? " asked Mr. Beck ; " what are his politics now ? "

" Don't know," said Tony.

" You don't know ! " echoed the other ; " oh ! " He shook his head archly. " You are very deep," he said. " There's a Tory meeting at Langstone this week : does Lord Lorrilaire take part ? "

" Don't know," said Tony.

" Then after all," said Mr. Beck, as if to himself, " after all Lord Lorrilaire is not a Conservative."

" Oh yes, he is," said Tony ; " all decent chaps are."

" Perhaps I am an indecent chap," said

Mr. Beck—"most interesting! Now that exercise of yours? Would you repeat it once for me?"

This request at once softened the heart of Tony and lulled to sleep his incipient suspicions. He began solemnly to rise and fall again and to accompany the movement with his mystic numbers. Suddenly he stopped short; something in the motions had brought back all his doubts. "I say," he said, "what have you been pumping me for? It's all private, you know."

"Nothing is private nowadays," said Mr. Beck, smiling, and with soft emphasis.

"Oh, but I say," said Tony, with a look as if he would collar him.

"I will come without a struggle," said Mr. Beck, setting out briskly again towards the house.

"Oh, but, you know," said Tony; "what are you going to do?"

"I am going to see Lord Lorrilaire."

"Yes; but what do you want with him?"

"I want to save him."

"Eh!"

"To save him. I am Beck." He stood still on the road and faced Tony. "I am Beck," he repeated.

"Good old Beck!" murmured Tony under his breath; but as he continued to stare with the same amazement, the other young man said again with his mild emphasis—

"I am Beck, of the *Rising Sun.*"

"Do you keep a public?" asked Tony, still wondering.

"Keep a public? Hah! Ho, ho, hah! Yes, by Heaven, I do! That is what I do. I keep a public, the great British public; and I keep them straight. Is it possible that you do not know the *Rising Sun*—the rising journal — the most influential (mark the word!) circulation in the world? I'll put you in it—with a sketch—here you are!"

During Tony's repetition of his performance Radley Beck had been busy with his note-book, and he now displayed to the eyes

of the astonished youth a lively sketch of a
figure with bent knees, done with a few
strokes of the pencil, and some notes added
by the same instrument. "Modern masher
—morning worship of goddess Hygeia—
Ninety-nine—the mystic number and the
expanded lung."

"Oh, by George! but——" began Tony.

"My other notes," continued Mr. Beck—
"here they are—Approaching marriage."

"But I never said there would be a
marriage," cried Tony.

"It doesn't matter," said Beck; "it brings
the matter to a point; it makes or mars. I
am a nineteenth-century Providence. And
it makes a paragraph too, and its contradiction
makes another."

"Good old Beck!" murmured Tony again,
with rising wonder.

They had begun again to move quickly
towards the house, and Tony, without thinking, led the way towards the window of his
room and began to enter. Mr. Beck watched

him with interest, and no sooner had his leader got in, than he followed him nimbly over the window-sill.

"A nice room," said Mr. Beck, when he had entered; "a bath? H—m—m!"

He looked at it with interest.

"It's for me," said Tony anxiously.

"All right!" said Beck cheerfully; "I don't want it. But look sharp; and, when you have done, I'll put myself to rights."

He seated himself easily on Tony's bed, and regarded him critically with his head on one side and his unruly forelock touching his thin black eyebrows.

Tony was much embarrassed. In spite of his experience of the world, he was essentially a modest boy, and he blushed at the thought of taking his bath under the aggressively observant eyes of this stranger. What if he were to see an account of his skin or figure in a number of the *Rising Sun*, or even a rude sketch of himself, sponge in hand? On the other hand, to make a fuss about the attendance of this person seemed to him absurd. He looked from his bath to his bed and back again with comical discomposure.

" Precisely," said the keen-eyed stranger ; " I see ; I will walk up and down on the terrace."

He slipped out of the window in a moment ; but Tony was hardly out of his bath before his visitor was in again, and again seated on the bed. Tony was annoyed, and the more annoyed to feel himself blushing.

" You must forgive me," said Beck crisply ; " it is such a chance to study the toilet of a masher."

" But I ain't a masher," said Tony, hurrying himself into some garments.

" That is what they all say," said Beck ; " that is the sign of the masher. If you were not one, you would be flattered at being called a masher—but those flannel under- clothes ? Surely they are peculiar."

" Oh yes," said Tony, zeal triumphing over modesty ; " they're medicated."

"Whose patent?" asked Beck, and he made some rapid notes of Mr. Fotheringham's answers, purposing in some spare hour to interview the ingenious patentee. Then the soap caught his eye, and he made a note of that and of the valuable properties which Mr. Fotheringham ascribed to it. Indeed, nothing escaped him : he tried the springs of the bed while he sat on it, and then crept under it to examine its mechanism from below. For very hurry Tony was slower than usual in his dressing. He felt as if all the furniture, his very clothes and even himself, were about to be put up to auction ; and, when at last he was dressed, he escaped with intense relief, though he left the stranger nimbly tripping about his room and using his favourite hair-brushes.

CHAPTER XIV.

No sooner had Tony escaped from the inquiring stranger than he made haste to find
his host and to warn him of his extraordinary
visitor.

"Never saw such a chap in my life," he
said; but when Archie heard that the new-
comer was Beck, he was vastly delighted, and
laughed aloud for joy.   That Beck should
have hit on Fotheringham seemed to him a
delightful chance, and full of humorous suggestions; and he knew in a moment, moreover, the cause of Beck's coming, and that
seemed to him a joke even more amusing.

"He's all right," he said; "he was a friend
of mine at Oxford; at least, we used to have
tremendous discussions.   And now he is sub-
editor of a brand-new paper, which is to show

up everybody for his good and put every-
thing to rights for the good of the universe.
You never saw such a fellow, Tony? No,
I'll bet you didn't. He used to tell us at
Oxford that his hat covered half the clever-
ness in England."

"Good old Beck!" cried Tony cheerfully.
After a minute he added thoughtfully, "His
hat's a doosid sight too big for him."

"Ah, but you see, his head grows so quick,"
said Archie; "the hat will fit him before
night."

"Oh, that's nonsense, you know," said
Tony, wagging his close-cropped head wisely.

Archie was going at once to greet his
former friend in Tony's room; but Tony
assured him that he would interrupt Mr.
Beck's toilet. They therefore went straight
to breakfast; and, when they entered the
breakfast-room, there was Mr. Radley Beck
with his back to the fire and his head on one
side, looking wiser than a magpie. His toilet
had not detained him long.

The rest of the guests assembled at Langley Castle were just settling themselves down to breakfast, some seated, others standing and inspecting the dishes on the side-table, but all obviously conscious of the presence of the remarkable stranger, who stood silent and smiling, and enchanted with the certainty that he was producing his effect. He loved to impress. He stood still silent and smiling, when Archie came in, and did not go forward to meet him. He only looked at him, as if he would instantly see through him without an effort.

"Well, Becky," said Archie, coming to him and shaking his limp hand heartily, "this is capital!"

"I hope so," said Beck, breaking his impressive silence with speech like a bird's chirping; "I had an hour or two to spare, and I came to say something to you."

"Out with it, then," said Archie; "or have your breakfast first;" and he propelled Mr. Beck towards the table, introducing him

by name, as he did so, to his other guests.
Mr. Beck gave little bows and quick glances
to right and left, and there was a general
movement of interest; but the little gentleman would have been genuinely surprised,
had he known that there was only one person
present, besides his host, to whom his name
suggested anything at all. This person was
Mr. Palfrey, who after a good look rose
from his chair and offered his large white
hand with a bland smile of comradeship,
while he said, as if in search of complete
certainty, "Mr. Beck, of the——" and here
he coughed, for he could not remember the
name of the particular organ of public opinion
with which the new-comer was connected.

"Yes," said Mr. Beck, looking sideways
and upwards at the eminent politician; "yes,
Mr. Palfrey, I am Beck, of the *Rising Sun.*"

"I am delighted to meet you at last," said
Mr. Palfrey; "I need not say that I have
long known you in print."

Mr. Beck emitted a slight purring noise.

Young Lord Lorrilaire was delighted by
the coming of this old acquaintance. He had
guessed in a moment that Beck, hearing of
the arrival of Lord Hackbut and Mr. Palfrey,
had started on the instant to prevent him
from being captured by the Conservative
party. It was so like Beck. Archie foresaw
much amusement in eluding both Lord Hackbut and Mr. Beck. It was a joke which
suited his present humour; and there was
only one person with whom he would share
it. He seized the first chance of speaking to
Dora alone, and was made even more happy
by her ready sympathy. Indeed, Dora was
content with the whole aspect of the game.
Elizabeth still kept her room, though her
mother stated curtly and with ill-concealed
chagrin that there was nothing the matter
with her. Lady Jane Lock's grimness was
itself strong evidence that Dora's side was
winning; and Lady Jane seemed to think it
hardly worth while, even in answer to her
host's questions, to try to make her child's

indisposition interesting. The truth is, that
Lady Jane was astounded by Elizabeth's
obstinacy, and half inclined to say that she
would not try to do a mother's duty to a
daughter so ungrateful. She was very red and
very upright ; and she would allow nothing
but arrowroot and nourishment of a like kind
to be sent up to Elizabeth, who was a young
lady of most healthy appetite; but, though
she maintained an appearance of firmness, she
was evidently despondent. And so Dora
Rutherford was well content, seeing that the
dangerous girl was sulking, as she said, in
her room, and that Archie for his part showed
no depression of spirits. And so, too, she
listened with rising pleasure to Archie's quick
sketch of the intentions of his political friends.
It all suited her game admirably well. The
young man's mind would be busy with politics
for that day at least; and therein was the
day's safety. She encouraged him to amuse
himself by dexterous evasions, and foresaw
amusement for herself, too, in the sight of the

sport and in the society of these interesting
men.

Lord Hackbut did not appear at breakfast;
but when he came downstairs he at once
asked for Lord Lorrilaire; and for a staunch
and uncompromising supporter of the Establishment, he showed a most strange annoyance at hearing that his young host had gone
to church. "What did he go there for?" he
said with a growl, which may have been an
oath. He was in a somewhat fiery humour,
not certain that there was not a threatening
of gout. At the sight of Mr. Beck regarding
him with his jackdaw air and his mysterious
smile, he uttered another growl, which may
have been a greeting, turned his back and
shut himself for the morning in the smoking-
room, of which he locked the door. He pretended to be deaf, when Beck soon afterwards
came and shook the handle.

Returning from church, Archie saw Beck
awaiting him on the terrace and Lord Hackbut's man at the front door. Beck came

hurrying, but had scarcely opened his mouth, when the servant presented Lord Hackbut's compliments and said that his lordship would take it as a kindness if his lordship would come and see his lordship in the smoking-room. With cheerful friendliness and an air of pleasing all parties, Archie passed his arm through Beck's, and with a nod to Dora, led his friend away to the smoking-room. He talked, as he led him, with a fine flow of words ; and when they were now close to the door of the smoking-room, he made a remark which he knew to be what he called a sure draw for Beck. So they entered the room both talking at once ; and Archie, shaking hands with Lord Hackbut, appealed to him to judge between them. The old lord re-mained silent, and looked at Mr. Beck with a very obvious intention ; and Radley Beck for his part hung his head on one side, smiled and remained. Archie, ignoring the desire of each, continued to chatter for a few minutes, and then seeming to remember suddenly a forgotten duty, uttered some words of apology as he fled, shut the door behind him, and left his two pursuers together.

At luncheon both Lord Hackbut and Mr. Beck appeared; but neither of them took part in the general conversation. Only, as the meal drew to a close, the old lord filled a pause by asking incisively across the table—"Mr. Peek, do you go back to town to-day?" And, as the other gentleman smiled and murmured "Beck," he added, "I hear that you brought no luggage with you."

"Oh, never mind that," cried Archie to Beck, for he, like everybody else, had stopped to listen; "I am sure Tony will lend you any amount of clothes."

Tony turned a face of amazement and comical indignation on his friend; and Beck began to shake his head.

"I am bound to be back to-night," he said, moving his little shoulders as if he were suddenly reminded of the weight of the world.

"But at least you'll stay to dinner," said Archie; "I am sure that Tony——"

"Oh, I say," said Tony; "yes, of course; I should be awfully glad," he added, "but really and truly I've only one dress suit, you know."

Nevertheless Archie insisted that Mr. Beck should return to the office of the *Rising Sun* by the latest train; and Mrs. Dormer's permission having been asked and obtained, it was settled that the sub-editor should dine in his morning clothes.

It now seemed as if Lord Hackbut had made up his mind to defer operations until after the departure of the irritating little man, whose presence increased the likelihood of an attack of gout, for, when luncheon was done, he betook himself again to solitude and an old volume of "Baily's Magazine," and made no further attempt to secure an interview with his host.

Beck, on the contrary, aware that his time was short, came straight to Lord Lorrilaire

and said, without preamble, that he had
come for a short talk and must have it.
Archie laughed and did not refuse; but he
led Mr. Beck with other of his guests through
all the gardens and hot-houses, and showed
him every horse in the stables, before he
would allow him to begin the confidential
talk; and when he did allow him to begin,
he displayed the most provoking flippancy,
making paradoxical excuses for the Conservative party, maintaining that it was more
liberal than the Liberal, and arguing that it
was absurd of the *Rising Sun*, or any other
organ or organist, to care a jot whether he,
Lord Lorrilaire, enrolled himself with "the
Ins" or "the Outs." Finally he attacked
Beck with great good-humour, reminding
him that he used to be an avowed disciple of
Mazzini, and asking him with what eyes the
great Italian patriot, the preacher of the
highest motives in political affairs, would
regard the methods and manners of the new
catch-penny or catch-halfpenny journalism.

Radley Beck shook his head but kept his temper, and made a few neat remarks in defence of his business ; but he gained no knowledge whatever of Lord Lorrilaire's present position or future intentions.

When the party met in the drawing-room before dinner, Archie found an opportunity and told Dora Rutherford of the success of his day ; but Dora was not so sure that his success was final. " Look ! " she said, directing his attention first to Lord Hackbut and then to Mr. Beck ; " neither of them looks a bit crestfallen ; they are both as pleased as Punch."

" That's because it's time for dinner," said Archie, and he went away smiling to offer his arm to Lady Jane Lock, and to ask after her daughter.

When they entered the dining-room, Dora found with keen pleasure that her place was between Lord Hackbut and Mr. Beck, who had taken her in. She found, as she had guessed, that both men were in great good-humour, and she promptly set herself the task of increasing their amiability. She knew by instinct that this was to be done by listening with intelligence and charm. Of the two men Lord Hackbut was by far the more attentive to his dinner; and Mr. Beck, whose favourite food and drink were bloaters and soda-water, was able to favour his charming neighbour with a little series of his choicest remarks. Naturally the first topic was the surprising fortune of Lord Lorrilaire, and Mr. Beck spoke neatly and tersely of the Archie Rayner of their Oxford days. Dora tried to draw from him his opinion of the transformed Lord Lorrilaire; but he slipped over the subject with a few general remarks. "What he needs now," he said, " is advertisement. He should hand himself over to me. With his wealth and name he only needs to be forced on the attention of the public, and there he is—or rather where isn't he? To blush unseen is an anachronism—it is contrary to the spirit of Democracy. Even the modest primrose has come out from the river's brim; it is a badge, a power; it is a great deal more than a primrose."

Dora murmured her doubt whether Archie would ever care to become prominent, and asked with an enchanting deference " if perhaps Archie would not do well to content himself with the duties and pleasures of a country gentleman." The sub-editor scouted the idea of a man of ability contenting himself with pottering about his property and riding after a fox. " All out of date," he said. " He must accept the democracy and exterminate the fox."

Dora gave a little cry of horror.

" Horses are an anachronism," said Beck, " at least as a means of locomotion. They will be the food of the democracy. To kill your own food for fun is atrocious in these days. Archie must give up the monotonous pheasant, and let the children go nutting in his woods."

" And mustn't a country gentleman shoot or ride any more ? " asked Dora.

"Certainly, if he wish to," said Mr. Beck, smiling upon the fair questioner ; "he can shoot glass balls and ride a tricycle."

"Oh!" cried Dora ; and "What's that?" asked Lord Hackbut, turning towards her with his most amiable grin.

"Mr. Beck says that the democracy will eat horses," she said.

"I should not wonder," said the old lord, who was as famous for his knowledge of horses as of the political situation; "and asses too," he added, with a most carnivorous grin.

Mr. Beck was enchanted by the fair lady, who listened to him with so keen an interest. Her manner of listening gave him a higher opinion of her cleverness than if she had dazed him with epigrams, and increased also with every moment his admiration of her beauty. He pressed upon her the names of his favourite photographers, and shook his head gravely at her contempt of a purely chemical notoriety.

"It is out of date," he said ; "my dear

lady; it is an anachronism, this absurd fear of the public, the generous, warm-hearted, inquisitive, enormous public. The Democracy wants beauty in the shop-windows. Be photographed! let me draw attention to you —a line—a paragraph. Permit the public to be interested in your personality."

He eyed her askance like a snake-charmer; but Dora would only laugh and shake her head in her turn.

"Write for me too," he said to her, when the moment had come for the ladies to go. "An occasional paragraph or sketch—'The world as seen by a woman of fashion!'—It would be enormous."

"Oh no! rather small, I think," said Dora, as she moved towards the door.

END OF VOL. I.

LONDON: PRINTED BY WILLIAM CLOWES AND SONS, LIMITED, STAMFORD STREET AND CHARING CROSS.